THE LAST OF THE JEDI

UNDERWORLD

By Jude Watson

SCHOLASTIC INC.
New York   Toronto   London   Auckland   Sydney
Mexico City   New Delhi   Hong Kong   Buenos Aires

www.starwars.com
www.scholastic.com

No part of this publication may be reproduced, stored in a retrieval system, or transmitted in any form or by any means, electronic, mechanical, photocopying, recording, or otherwise, without written permission of the publisher. For information regarding permission, write to Scholastic Inc., Attention: Permissions Department, 557 Broadway, New York, NY 10012.

ISBN-13: 978-0-439-68136-0
ISBN-10: 0-439-68136-7

Copyright © 2005 Lucasfilm Ltd. & ™. All Rights Reserved. Used Under Authorization.

Cover art by John Van Fleet

SCHOLASTIC and associated logos are trademarks and/or registered trademarks of Scholastic Inc.

17 16 15 14 13 12 11 10 9 8   9 10 11 12/0

Printed in the U.S.A.
First printing, December 2005

CHAPTER ONE

Glimpsed through a curtain of cold gray rain, the ruined Jedi Temple looked more like a trick of the eye than a once-magnificent structure. To Ferus Olin, the Temple appeared to be a ghost image, like an afterburn on a vidscreen. He blinked. He felt as though the entire structure was dissolving before his eyes.

Since the end of the Clone Wars, so much in his life had seemed not real and hyper-real at the same time. He knew it wasn't logical, but it made sense to him. One moment he had been leading a peaceful life on a pleasant world, and the next he was a resistance fighter, then a prisoner, then a fugitive. And with each new twist and turn, he found himself wondering: *How did this happen?*

Get a grip, Ferus, he told himself now. He was here, and he had a job to do. The Temple was all too real, occupied by Imperial stormtroopers.

He'd absorbed the shock of the Empire occupying the Temple. Except that seeing it was like being punched in the gut. The Temple looked somehow terrible to him, like a being that had received a mortal wound.

He had once been a Jedi apprentice. He had left the Jedi, but step-by-step he was managing to reclaim what he'd lost — the same pure connection to the Force, the same allegiance to his fellow Jedi — or, now, the memory of them. Seeing the Temple like this hurt the deepest part of him.

"Ferus? Don't know whether you've noticed? But it's raining."

Ferus turned to his companion, Trever Flume. The thirteen-year-old's teeth were chattering. The hood he'd pulled over his bluish hair hadn't done much to keep him dry. A drop of rain rolled off the tip of his hood and hit his nose.

"Rain" was putting it mildly. Now Ferus felt his sodden cloak, his clammy skin. Part of his Jedi training had been to learn how to be impervious to physical discomfort. Feel the rain, feel the cold, then let it go. But he hadn't been a Jedi in a long time, and he had to admit he was freezing.

"Not that I'm complaining," Trever said through clenched teeth. "But I can't feel my fingers. Or my feet. And I'm hungry. There are icicles on my hair. And I'm —"

"Right. I get the point," Ferus said. "Just a few more minutes."

"Fine. If my toes fall off, just alert me, okay? Stick 'em in my pocket or something."

Ferus shook his head. He couldn't seem to lose Trever. The boy had stowed away on Ferus's escape ship from Bellassa, and it had taken Ferus a few weeks to realize that Trever wasn't going away. He was a smart, resourceful kid, but Ferus still wasn't crazy about taking him along. Ferus had given him the option to leave, but Trever hadn't taken it. Ferus didn't quite know what to do with him, and until he figured it out, he and Trever were stuck together. Trever had street skills and a kind of stubbornness that could morph into courage. There were times when Ferus was actually glad to have him along.

Ferus peered through the electrobinoculars again. The Temple was definitely being used. It had taken him only a few hours in Coruscant to pick up the gossip on the street. The Empire was using the Temple as a prison for captured Jedi. There were whispers that some had survived, that some had returned to the Temple before the homing beacon was dismantled. There they had found stormtroopers and an Imperial prison where their home had been.

That was the rumor, anyway.

Ferus didn't know how much of it was true.

Obi-Wan Kenobi had told him that he'd managed to transform the homing beacon into a warning beacon before any Jedi had returned. That didn't match the Empire's story. So part of the rumor was a lie. Even if some Jedi had returned, there couldn't be many of them. Ferus knew that almost all had been killed in the purge.

But even if there was only one, he had to get in and see.

He already suspected who was inside: Fy-Tor-Ana, the Jedi known for her grace with a lightsaber. Ferus had rescued the great Jedi Master Garen Muln in the caves of Illum, and Garen had told him how Fy-Tor had left him and promised to return. She'd been heading for the Temple and had never come back.

She had to be here. If she'd been free, she would have returned to Garen. Ferus could only conclude that she was either imprisoned or dead.

Garen himself was recovering on a hidden asteroid that Ferus hoped to set up as a new Jedi base. He didn't know how many Jedi might be alive, but they would need a safe place to live.

He noted the comings and goings of Imperial ships. Since the old hangar had been destroyed, they'd built a new landing platform off the once-grand front plaza. It protruded like an ugly scar.

Don't think of what was. Think of the next step.

So, it was a prison. He knew prisons.

It was difficult to break out. But not as difficult to break *in.*

"I know what you're thinking," Trever said as he stamped his boots to warm his feet. "You're thinking we can do it."

"Well, we can."

"Yeah. Sure. No problem. What's a couple hundred stormtroopers?"

Ferus kept his gaze on the Temple. "I have an advantage."

"Besides me?" Trever smirked.

"They might occupy the Temple, but they don't *know* the Temple. No one knows it like a Jedi. I can get us in — and get us out."

"So you say."

Ferus gave him a level look. "Listen, I can do this alone. I'd rather do it alone. We can have a rendezvous point —"

"No." Trever's voice was flat. "I'm with you."

They'd already had the argument. Trever saw the shift in Ferus's gaze that meant he'd accepted the inevitable. "So how do you figure we'll get in?" the boy asked.

"I think I have a way," Ferus said. "We drop from

a ship straight onto the burned tower. I can see a place where part of the tower was blasted away. That will give us some footing. Directly above there used to be a small, glassed-in garden on the south side. It was used to grow herbs for the kitchen. If we can climb over that blasted part into where the garden used to be, we can get into a service hallway. There was a system of linkage service tunnels that ran to the service turbolifts. With any luck some of the tunnels have survived, and we can get into the lower levels that way. That's the only place the prison could be."

"What ship are you talking about?" Trever asked. "We left Toma's star cruiser at that landing platform. Besides, if we're both going in, who's going to drive?"

"We're not going to use Toma's cruiser." Toma was a new ally. He'd just fought a battle against Imperial forces on his home planet of Acherin. He and his first officer, Raina, had joined forces with Ferus and Obi-Wan. Obi-Wan had returned to his mysterious exile, but Raina and Toma had remained on the asteroid to watch Garen. "I've got a different idea. We'll hire an air taxi."

"You mean, jump in an air taxi and say, 'Hey, driver, could you please drop us on the tower?'"

"Well, it has to be the right driver."

"Okay, let's review," Trever said. "We're going to

drop from a moving vehicle onto a ruined tower to find a maybe-opening that *could* lead to some blasted-to-bits tunnels, in order to maybe-make it into a place flooded with stormtroopers so we can maybe-rescue one Jedi who, if we're lucky, might still be alive."

Ferus looked Trever right in the eye. "You have a problem with that?"

"Nah," Trever said. "Let's go."

Many things had changed in Coruscant, but some things remained the same. On one of the lower levels of Galactic City there was still a shadowy landing platform where private air taxi drivers could be hired to do illegal and dangerous trips, no questions asked. While Ferus negotiated with a squat, muscular humanoid with tattooed facial markings, Trever found a food stand that looked like it might not poison him. He quickly devoured a veg turnover and downed a carton of juice. When Ferus beckoned, he stuffed another turnover in his pocket and was ready to go.

They climbed into the back of a battered air taxi and zoomed through the colorful laserlights of the entertainment district. The driver kept to the prescribed space lanes — for now. As he snaked his way up through the levels to the Senate district, they could see the ruined Temple better and better.

Here the space lanes were crowded with traffic. The driver slid smoothly into the flow. He kept the engines powered down, but at the last moment he veered off into a lane closer to the Temple. He dived down and around the damaged tower and hung in the air.

"Go if you're going," he grunted. "In a moment I'll be on Imperial sensors."

Ferus activated a liquid cable line and turned to Trever. He saw the boy pale.

"It will hold you," Ferus reassured him. "And I'll be right next to you."

Trever swallowed, then nodded. Ferus hooked the second line to his belt.

Ferus released both liquid cables himself, aiming for a spot above a jagged edge of the tower that looked like it would hold them. The line caught and jerked them forward roughly as the driver accelerated. Ferus cursed the driver in his head for the premature boost as they flew wildly through the air, the wind whistling against their ears. Rain pelted their faces like sharp needles. Ferus landed hard on the protruding edge and grabbed for Trever to guide his landing. Trever smacked against the tower and hugged it.

"That was fun," he croaked.

"Just don't look down."

"I'll try not to."

The air taxi zoomed off, merging seamlessly back into the flow of heavy traffic. The whole operation had taken seconds.

Ferus wiped the rain out of his eyes. From his position on the tower, a good deal of Galactic City was spread out below him. He could see the sprawl of the Senate complex and the new, massive statue of Emperor Palpatine that Palpatine himself had commissioned. From here, Ferus and Trever were invisible to the Imperial traffic heading to the new landing platform, but he couldn't rely on it for long.

Ferus felt the rough stone of the Temple against his back. Sure, he would have to break in, but a surge of feeling rose in him, a connection like no other.

He was home.

CHAPTER TWO

A flexible durasteel arm of a sensor was still sticking out of the wall. Ferus tested his weight on it, and it held. Using it as leverage, he was able to hook his fingers over the edge above and boost himself up for a quick look at the site of the old garden.

With a grunt, Ferus balanced on his palms. The garden hadn't just succumbed to the fire, he saw — it had been blasted. Chunks of blackened stone blocked the former entrance. The glass had shattered and needles of it were still lying about.

He remembered. . . .

Standing next to Siri as she crushed an herb and held it under his nose. "What does it say to you?"

"It's an herb," he said.

"But what does it say?"

"I don't understand, Master." What did she want? Ferus was only thirteen, just beginning

his apprenticeship. He was afraid all the time of doing or saying the wrong thing.

"This is part of the Force, too, Ferus. Connection to living things. Close your eyes. Smell. Good. Now. What does it say?"

"It says . . . lunch."

Siri barked her short laugh. "Not very imaginative, but I guess it will have to do. Let's try another. . . ."

"Master? Yoland Fee doesn't like anyone to pick his herbs. It's a rule for the Padawans."

Siri turned to him, her hands full of edible flowers and green herbs. She smiled.

"You know, Ferus, if you could manage to get some of that starch out of your tunic, we'd get along much better."

Ferus felt the strain shoot through his arms from holding himself up. He dropped back to his perch. He hadn't fully realized that entering the Temple put him at risk from more than Imperial troops. He'd take stormtroopers over memories any day.

Siri had been right, of course. Thinking back to that moment, he remembered how careful he'd been to keep his spine straight, his gaze level. He had been conscious of his every word, tailoring it to what the perfect apprentice should say or do.

Every time Ferus looked back to a memory of

himself as a Padawan, he wondered how anyone could stand him. It was only later, on Bellassa, through his friendship with Roan Lands, that he had learned to unbend from the rigid contours he had set for himself, to see that perfection was a prison he had built that kept him apart from others.

He missed his old life with Roan as much as he missed the Jedi. War and the Empire had torn his life in two, as it had for so many in the galaxy. At first he hadn't recognized the change. Palpatine's grab for power had been so slow, so careful. So fiendishly smart. He had known that in times of turmoil beings looked for leadership — and didn't examine too closely what that leadership was up to. When the reality behind the mask emerged, it was too late.

"The stones have collapsed around the opening," he told Trever. "We'll have to blast one. Think you can manage it?"

"I thought you'd never ask."

He had discovered that Trever was something of an explosives expert. Trever could calmly take apart an alpha charge and amp it or weaken its power without batting an eye. His brother Tike had been part of the resistance movement on Bellassa and had taught him. Tike had died, along with Trever's father, at the hands of the Empire. After that, Trever had made his living on the streets of Bellassa, and had picked up plenty of knowledge on the way. He was a product of war and suffering, old before his time, hiding the vulnerabilities of a boy that still crouched underneath his bravado.

"We'll need a half charge, just enough to blow a small hole," Ferus told Trever. "We don't want to attract any attention."

Trever fished an alpha charge out of his utility belt. "This should do it. Boost me up."

Ferus gave him a boost. He held onto the boy's feet as Trever wriggled, positioning the charge between the massive stones.

"Let's take cover," Ferus said, easing Trever back down.

"It's only a half charge."

The blast almost blew Ferus off the ledge. He grabbed at the protruding sensor and swung in mid-air, caught by a buffeting wind. It grabbed at his body and twirled it like a reed. He decided to take his own advice to Trever and not look down.

He swung his legs back onto his old perch. Trever had squeezed himself into the carved-out opening.

"That was a half charge?" Ferus asked, incredulous.

"It's not an exact science, you know," Trever replied sheepishly.

"Let's just hope the stormtroopers didn't hear it. Come on."

Ferus boosted himself up once more to inspect Trever's handiwork. Despite the power of the blast, the hole was small, a testament to the strength of the stone. It was just big enough to squeeze through.

Well, that takes care of one of my fears, anyway, Ferus thought. They wouldn't be stranded on this tower. At least they could get inside.

He wouldn't think about how they would get out. Yet.

Ferus Force-leaped up to the opening and balanced. He reached a hand down for Trever and hauled him up. They bent over and eased through the opening Trever had blasted through the stone.

They were inside the Temple now, in a place Ferus knew well, but he found himself lost for a moment. This bore no resemblance to the Temple he'd known. He was in a heavily damaged area, and for a moment he couldn't get his bearings. One wall was demolished, another blackened with smoke. The corridor he'd expected to turn into was gone. Instead there was a mountain of rubble.

"We'll have to go this way," he said, turning in the opposite direction.

They climbed over a collapsed wall. Ferus stood still for a moment. Despite all that had happened, the Force remained present. It was still here for him, and he connected to it.

Suddenly, he felt completely oriented, and very clear.

The Temple could be a gigantic maze to outsiders, but to a Jedi the design made sense. It had been fashioned to conform to the life of a Jedi, to make getting around easy. So it followed the rhythms of a Jedi, with meditation flowing into physical activity into nature into food into study into research and support.

"This used to be the droid repair area," Ferus told Trever. "So there should be an access to the service tunnels here, too."

Pools of water had collected on the floor. Rain dripped in. The smell of smoke rose from the blackened walls. Ferus tried to push any emotion away. He needed to focus.

"I like to look at the droids," Anakin said.

Ferus nodded. He had come to drop off a small droid for repair as a favor to a Jedi Master. To his surprise, he'd found Anakin Skywalker checking over droid parts.

He didn't know Anakin very well. He'd only just arrived at the Temple this past year. He'd heard the rumors, of course. How strong Anakin was in the Force, how Qui-Gon Jinn had picked him off a remote desert planet. How Obi-Wan Kenobi had offered to train him personally after Qui-Gon's death. How he could be the Chosen One.

"I built a droid on my homeworld," Anakin said. Something in his voice told Ferus that Anakin was lonely.

Ferus wished he had the ability to say the right thing, to respond with warmth to a boy he didn't know. He wished his awkwardness didn't come off as stiffness. He wished he were more like Tru Veld or Darra Thel-Tanis, who could talk to anyone and become their friend. But it was hard for him to know what to say. He didn't have that gift. His teachers were always telling him to be more in touch with the Living Force.

"I don't remember my homeworld," he said finally. "Or my family."

Anakin looked at him under a shock of blond hair. "Then you're lucky."

That lonely boy had grown into an astoundingly gifted Jedi. And now he was dead. Ferus didn't know how or where. He'd been reluctant to ask Obi-Wan. The look on the Jedi Master's face when Anakin was mentioned was enough to stop Ferus. Grief had marked Obi-Wan, and he looked older and grayer than his age would warrant.

Ferus was beginning to make sense of the blackened and twisted shapes now. There, the heap of fused durasteel — that had been the shelving that had run along one wall. It had held droid parts. Stone had crumbled into pebbles that crunched under Ferus's boots as he walked into the echoing space. He kicked through some melted parts on the floor. Gaping holes in the roof overhead had let in the morning rain. Rustlings told him that creatures were living here, scurrying through the debris.

The protocol droids were eerie shapes, half melted, their eye sockets blank. They looked like fallen soldiers.

The smell of decay was in his nostrils. Decay and failure and ruin.

And it was only the beginning of what he would see.

"So where's the entrance to the tunnels?" Trever asked.

Ferus wrenched his mind back to the task at hand. He gazed about, trying to orient himself. "That opening there leads to the grand hall. I think we'd better avoid it. The entrance to the service tunnels was over there. At least, I think that's where it was."

They stared across the room at a gigantic pile of rubble.

"All I can say is, if we have to get through that, you'd better be right," Trever said.

Suddenly they heard the noise of tramping feet.

"Stormtroopers," Trever whispered.

Ferus quickly pointed to a towering, misshapen pile of twisted metal. It had fused from the heat; it had once been a pile of droids. The jagged nature of the heap had created holes throughout. They would be able to squeeze inside and hide underneath it.

Just in time. A squad of white-armored stormtroopers entered the space through the blasted-out opening that led to the grand hall. The officer in charge spoke through his headset. "Sensors indicate life-form activity."

Trever looked at Ferus, alarmed. Ferus watched as the squad began to systematically comb the space, quadrant by quadrant. That was the trouble with stormtroopers, he thought testily. They were so *efficient.*

Within minutes they would spot them. Ferus had no doubt of that. They were circling the droid heaps, checking every crevice, every dark corner.

Ferus felt something wet and bristling brush his leg. Only the most severe discipline of the Jedi, ingrained in his bones, prevented him from flinching. A meer rat, fat and bold, waddled by. Before Ferus could warn him, Trever jumped slightly, banging his head against the metal. The faintest clang sounded through the space.

"Halt activity." The officer swiveled, training a glow-rod just centimeters from their hiding place. "Evidence of intruders. Search and destroy."

CHAPTER THREE

Trever reached into his pocket. Without making a sound, he withdrew the turnover he'd placed there. He tossed it a short distance away. The meer rat scudded after it.

The officer caught the movement. The light from the glow rod was jerked toward the sound, and it caught the rat in mid-scurry.

"Another rat," the stormtrooper said in disgust. "They're so big they trip the sensors. I'm getting tired of these false alarms. Come on, let's head out."

Ferus and Trever waited until the sound of the footsteps faded.

"That was close," Ferus said.

"And there goes the rest of my lunch," Trever added.

They wriggled out. Avoiding the rat munching on the turnover, they headed toward the area where Ferus was sure they'd find the entrance to the tunnels. The debris was piled so high that there was no way to tell where the entrance had been. He closed his eyes.

Ferus concentrated on the memory of his brief conversation with Anakin as a boy. He used an exercise that every Padawan had learned. They were led to a spot, told to open their eyes, look for five seconds, then close them again. Then they were to describe everything they'd seen. Sometimes they faced what seemed to be a blank wall, and they would have to note every crevice, every irregularity.

Ferus reached back, past years of events and feelings that could cloud his mind, past his child's perspective, and focused on what he had seen. He could conjure up the texture of the cold against his fingers, the droid parts neatly labeled on the shelves, the banks of computers. When he remembered the ding on the dome of a battered astromech droid to Anakin's right, he knew he was getting there. The Force helped him to connect to memory as much as what was around him now.

He calculated the distance. He remembered how high the entrance had been, how many meters above his head. He remembered his own height and made the necessary calculations.

Then he walked forward. "It's behind here," he said, pointing to a spot in the pile. His Jedi memory and the Force had guided him.

Either that, or he was completely wrong. It wouldn't be the first time.

He unsheathed the lightsaber that had been given to him by Garen Muln in the caves of Illum. From the first moment, it had felt as if it had always belonged in his hand. He inserted the lightsaber and slowly rotated it until its heat started to dissolve the area around it in an ever growing circle. Trever stepped forward, fascinated as always by a lightsaber's power.

When Ferus had cleared enough space, he pushed aside the rest of the rocks and debris with his hands and crawled in, holding a glow rod in front of him. He could sense, rather than see, that he'd unblocked the entrance. He called back to Trever to follow him. He had to crawl for about twenty meters, but at last he passed through and was able to stand. Trever joined him seconds later.

It was difficult to get their footing due to the debris and dirt that littered the walkway. This had once been a gleaming white tunnel, lit by pale blue glowlamps. It had been built to transport droids from repair to various points in the Temple. The ceiling was low and the walls curved around.

"This comes out near the living quarters," Ferus said. "That part of the Temple, from what I can see, wasn't as badly destroyed as the others."

"That means we'll be bumping into more storm-troopers," Trever said.

"I'll do my best to avoid them." Ferus slowly moved through the tunnel. "The Padawans used to explore all the service tunnels and little-used passageways. Sometimes it was helpful if you didn't want to bump into any of your teachers if you'd forgotten an assignment or had skipped a practice session."

"Aw, Ferus, you've lived up to my expectations. I knew you were the kind of renegade who didn't do his homework."

Ferus snorted. Trever was way off base. Trever knew a different person from what Ferus had been. "Renegade" hardly fit the description of his Padawan years. Actually, he had never skipped an assignment or a practice session. He had striven for perfection in every waking moment. He was driven by his need to excel. As a result, he hadn't made friends easily. It was only near the end of his apprenticeship that he had grown close to Darra and Tru.

Darra had died on Korriban. He still felt responsible for her death. He had left the Jedi Order because of it.

And there was Anakin. Anakin, whose gifts were so great, who had thought of Ferus as a rival. He remembered their squabbles now, and their deep rift. He would have done things differently now. He would not have judged Anakin the way he did. Now Anakin was dead, along with Tru, along with the Padawans he'd lived with for most of his childhood. Even the greatest warriors of the Jedi — Mace Windu, Kit Fisto, even Yoda — could not defeat the Sith.

So what made him think that *he* could?

I know I can't defeat them. But maybe if we strike enough blows, we can hurt them.

It wasn't in the Jedi nature to act out of anger. But was it really so wrong to enter a fight because you were so deeply and thoroughly enraged?

Ferus held up a hand as they approached the end of the tunnel. He knew that it opened into a service passageway that ran parallel to one of the main halls. He was betting that the stormtroopers would use the main halls, which were larger and led to the grand staircases and turbolifts. The service passageways were narrow and had a complicated layout. It was easy to get lost.

"Where do you think the prison is?" Trever asked in a low tone.

"It has to be in the big storage rooms," Ferus replied. "It's one of the only places that could be reconfigured into a secure area. And from what I could see through the electrobinoculars, it remains largely intact. There was a series of turbolifts at the end of the first service passageway that led down to the storage floor. With any luck they'll still be there. Even if they aren't functioning, we might be able to get down one of the shafts."

Waiting a moment to ensure that the service passageway was empty, Ferus edged out into the hall. Trever followed as he held the glow rod in front of him, keeping it down to its lowest setting. Here the walls were also blackened from the fire, but the hallway didn't seem too badly damaged.

Only a wall separated them from a main passageway, and they could hear the noise of activity on the other side.

"I don't get it," Ferus murmured. "There seems to be a lot of movement. This place must be more than a prison. No wonder there was so much activity at the landing platform."

"The more the merrier," Trever said grimly.

Ferus reached the turbolift area. He frowned in disappointment. What had been a turbolift bank was now a collapsed heap of duracrete. Even worse, it blocked the connection to the other service hallways.

"We're going to have to use the main hallway," he said. "Just for a bit, to get to the other turbolift bank."

He paused in front of a door. He heard no sound, so he cautiously eased it open. The hallway was empty. Ferus knew exactly where he was. If he followed this hall to the right, it would lead him to the Room of a Thousand Fountains. Beyond that was another passage that would get him closer.

Beckoning to Trever, he emerged into the hallway. Moving quickly and silently, they hurried down the hall. As they passed the large wooden doorway to the Room of a Thousand Fountains, Ferus's footsteps faltered.

"What is it?" Trever whispered.

"One moment."

He couldn't help himself. It had been his favorite place in the Temple. He had to see. Ferus pushed open the doors.

He took a cautious step inside. The first thing that struck him was the silence. In his mind he'd been expecting the calming note of splashing, trickling water. He had even turned his face upward to feel the cooling spray.

Empty. Desolate. The remains of the fragrant plants and flowers, dried, brown. Stumps rising like crooked fingers. Dried pond beds, stone urns upturned and cracked.

He turned. He would have to harden his heart against this. He couldn't allow every sight to be a blow. It would just slow him down.

They walked past the Map Room, where once a student could access any quadrant of the galaxy, any world. Ferus wasn't tempted to peek. And Jocasta Nu's beloved library — without even entering, he could see through the blasted doors that it had been systematically destroyed. All that knowledge, all that wisdom — gone.

Gone.

But I must keep moving.

They heard footsteps behind them. Ferus yanked Trever behind a tall column.

He pressed himself against the column as the footsteps drew closer.

It was some kind of Imperial messenger and an officer.

"You were supposed to be here this morning."

"It took some time to gather the data."

"Well, you're here now. Take it to the Inquisitor's office."

"Location?"

"Follow this hallway and go through the double doors. It's the first door on your right, the one with the windows. Then put it down and leave. Inquisitor Malorum isn't here."

Malorum? At the Temple?

This could be either a disaster or a piece of good luck. Obi-Wan had asked Ferus to discover what Malorum was up to, if he could. And it sounded like Malorum's office was right here, in the Temple.

Of course, Malorum knew his face. Not only that, he hated him. Lucky for Ferus that he wasn't here.

Ferus thought back to the directions the officer had given.

It can't be. Malorum's office is Yoda's living quarters?

"He's not expected back until tomorrow. He'll expect everything to be in order then. He's going to move the base of operations over here from the Imperial Stronghold. . . ."

The words faded as the footsteps did.

"Not that guy again," Trever moaned softly. He had known Malorum, too, on Bellassa. It was Malorum who had put a death mark on Trever's head.

"Yeah, he keeps turning up, doesn't he?" Why would be put his office in the Temple? And why choose, out of all the hundreds of rooms, Yoda's private quarters?

Because he can.

The arrogance!

They started down the hallway again. It was empty, and they hurried to the bank of turbolifts and jumped inside. Ferus's heartbeat quickened. At last he would discover if any Jedi remained alive.

CHAPTER FOUR

The turbolift worked smoothly. It was a piece of luck. It descended all the way down to the storage floor and opened. Ferus was prepared, his lightsaber at the ready, for whatever would lie on the other side of the door. But it opened onto an empty hallway.

He took a cautious step forward. Not only empty, but . . . *dusty*.

He listened for sound, for movement. He brought the Force to him and sent it out. True, his Force sense was still rusty at times, but he received nothing. Surely if this were a prison, he would pick up echoes of the Living Force, no matter how faint. Especially from Jedi.

"You look worried," Trever whispered. "And when you worry, I worry."

"I don't *feel* anything," Ferus said.

"Is that all?"

"For a Jedi, that's everything."

They moved forward cautiously. Ferus wasn't as familiar with this area as he was with others. They were on the very lowest levels of the Temple now. All Padawans were required to take an extensive tour of the Temple, from top to bottom, and become familiar with the layout, but Ferus had only visited the storage areas infrequently.

Luckily it was a standard layout, just parallel hallways leading to storage rooms of varying sizes. They walked down, peering into one after the other.

Empty.

Empty except for scattered bins, random items stored here and not raided because they weren't valuable — towels, tarps. Soap. Glow rods and servodrivers. Blankets.

"I guess the Empire found the treasure," Trever said. "But maybe they overlooked something? Anything down here?"

"What treasure?" Ferus asked.

"The treasure the Jedi had," Trever said. "You know the Order was rich. All those payments from worlds they protected . . ."

Ferus was furious. "That was a lie told by the Emperor. The Jedi never took payment for their services. Palpatine was trying to turn the galaxy against the Jedi to justify his crimes. And now you're repeating the lies!"

"Hey, Ferus, power down. How was I supposed to know it was a lie? Everyone said it."

"Everyone says the Emperor is on your side, too."

"Excellent point."

In many ways, this was the worst fallout from Order 66, the one that had destroyed the Jedi. History had been rewritten. Palpatine's lies had changed how the galaxy thought of the Jedi. Their lives of service had become bids for power. Their selflessness had become greed.

"I'm sorry," Trever said, looking at the expression on his face. "I hear the word 'treasure' and I start to salivate heavily. You know me. . . ." He tried to smile, but his eyes were worried. "You forget I'm a thief."

"Not anymore," Ferus said. The moment of anger passed. He looked around. "I don't understand. This is the logical place for the prison. And the word on the street is that the Jedi are down deep in the Temple storerooms."

"Is there anywhere else they could be keeping them?"

Ferus shook his head. "Anything is possible, but . . ." He stopped. Just as they passed the largest storeroom, he thought he'd caught a glint of a reflection. Cautiously, he walked forward. There was no Living Force here. But there was . . . something.

He raised his glow rod.

It took him a moment to make sense of the piles, the jumble of objects. Rows and rows and rows disappearing in the dusky light at the corners of the vast space.

Lightsabers.

Ferus felt his breath catch and his heart stop. He could not move.

Trever, sensing his emotion, drew back. In a rare display of tact, he said nothing.

Ferus moved forward. His boot hit a lightsaber hilt, and he flinched. He leaned over to pick it up. He ran his fingers along the hilt. He didn't recognize it. He put it carefully back down.

Row after row after row . . . jumbles and piles, some laid out neatly, no doubt for identification.

"How many?" he whispered.

He leaned over to pick up a hilt here, another there.

Here was the proof. The Empire must have collected the lightsabers when they could, but for what purpose, he wasn't sure. To identify Jedi, perhaps. But who would be able to recognize the hilts but another Jedi? Or perhaps they meant to study the lightsabers in order to be able to use them as weapons one day.

After all, Obi-Wan had told him that Emperor

Palpatine was a Sith. Darth Vader was his apprentice. Did they want to build a Sith army?

But what did it matter? There was a pounding inside him, metal against rock. Something fierce and elemental. Grief was pounding him.

This is how it worked, he realized. *Each time you think you have comprehension of your sorrow, you get blindsided again. You slide back into your rage and your disbelief.*

"All of them," he said, walking on. "So many."

And each one represented a noble life, gone.

And then he saw what he dreaded — the light-saber of someone he loved.

He picked it up. He knew it well. He had even tried to fix it. Little had he known then that a favor for a friend would end up being the beginning of the end of his career as a Jedi.

Tru Veld had been his friend. Tru had been everyone's friend. His silver eyes, his gentleness, the way he would start a conversation in the middle and circle around to the beginning. The way he had been the one to see past Ferus's stiff manner into his heart.

He didn't know what to do with the lightsaber. He couldn't bear to leave it. But, gazing around, Ferus realized that Tru would want it to lie with the others. He placed it gently back down.

Some stormtrooper, some officer, some feature-less clone, some brutal weapon, from the air or the ground, had cut down the brimming life and gener-ous heart of Tru Veld. To the Empire he had been just another score, another Jedi down. Another step toward their goal. To Ferus, he had been full of complexities and ideas and hopes and passions and will. He'd been unique and fully alive. The fact that he was gone — here it was again, that feeling of something being too real, and yet impossible at the same time.

"Ferus," Trever said urgently. "I hear some-thing."

And he should have heard it, too, if the roar of sorrow hadn't been in his ears.

A squad of stormtroopers, by the sound of it.

He whirled around, his gaze searching for what he should have known was there.

"A silent alarm," he said.

He knew the way they worked, the Imperials. He'd fought them for months on Bellassa. He should have known this.

"*They* spread the rumors," he said. "They want everyone to think this is a Jedi prison. They know that any Jedi left alive will come." He turned back to Trever. "Now I understand. This isn't a prison. It's a trap."

CHAPTER FIVE

There had to be another way out. There always was, even in storage areas like this one. Ferus knew that the Temple had been designed with an eye toward utility as well as beauty. Energy must be conserved, even physical energy. This space was too vast to have only one way to unload cargo.

"Follow me," he whispered to Trever. Instead of leaving by the front door, they ran down the aisle, past the lightsabers, past the memories and the sorrow, to the very back of the room. There he found what he was looking for — an entrance to the service tunnels. This should lead them back to the hallway.

First problem: The tunnel was sealed with a door, and the old control panel didn't work.

Silently and swiftly, Ferus sliced through the door with his lightsaber. It would leave evidence of their presence, but it was too late to do anything else. He could hear the squad now at the very front of the room. Any moment now they would be discovered.

Trever didn't need an invitation. He bolted through the hole Ferus had created. Ferus followed and they ran down the service tunnel. As he ran, Ferus calculated where the tunnel was taking them. It made a sharp right turn, and he knew that they were now running parallel to the second service hallway.

"If we can get out somewhere along here, we can make it to the turbolift," he told Trever.

"And go where?"

"Well, anywhere but here is an option."

Ferus saw a control panel up ahead and, faintly, the outline of a door. He tried the control panel and this time it worked. The door slid open. Good. This way, once the stormtroopers entered the service tunnel, they wouldn't be able to pinpoint where Ferus and Trever had left it. It slid shut behind them.

They were in another storage room, which Ferus had expected. This one was filled with empty shelves. As they ran toward the door, Ferus suddenly stopped.

"Ferus, come on!"

He bent down and ran his finger along the shelf. "Look. They left marks."

"What left marks?"

"The bins. This was a food storage area." He sniffed. "You can still smell the dried herbs." *There's one for you, Siri. You knew it would come in handy.*

"Fascinating. Now can we continue escaping?"

Ferus was thinking fast, remembering. "Dry food storage had a separate delivery system. If the cooks ran out of anything, they could plug in what they needed on tech screens in the kitchen and the information would be transferred down here. Droids would monitor the readouts, find the items, and carry them to vertical lifts. The lifts run on compressed air. They would shoot the cans up to the food halls, where they'd be held in a temporary zero-gravity immersion — in other words, in midair. The lifts are small, but we might be able to squeeze in — that is, if the compressed air system still works." While he spoke, Ferus was quickly checking the control panel.

"You mean you're going to blast me up on thin air?" Trever didn't seem sure of *that*.

"You'll have the ride of your life."

"Can I remind you that I'm not a can of beans?"

"We're in luck. It still works."

"Hey, what happens if the zero-gravity part doesn't work?"

"Look for a handhold on your way down. Trever,

it's the only way to escape the stormtroopers. They'll never figure it out."

"This just keeps getting better and better," Trever groaned. But he squeezed himself into the small vertical lift, tucking his knees under his chin. "By the way, have you given any thought to how we're going to get out of the Temple?"

"I'm thinking."

"That doesn't sound very promising."

"I don't make promises. Only plans."

"It's a pleasure doing business with you, Ferus."

"One last thing — if I can't make it, try to make it to the landing platform and steal a ship. Meet me back at the asteroid."

He shut the door on Trever's incredulous look. The *whoosh* of air told him that the transport had succeeded.

Ferus crossed to the next lift tube. He flattened himself and twisted, but he could not fit himself into the opening. He slammed his head and bumped his elbow as he tried to jam himself in.

Wait, Ferus.

He focused on remembering.

Siri bent down to help him. He had fallen during a routine hike, just because he hadn't been paying attention. Fallen from a boulder, straight down, and hit the dirt.

First her expert hands made sure he was all

right. Then she leaned back on her heels, balancing expertly despite the fact that they'd been hiking for six hours in rugged terrain.

"When you felt yourself falling, why didn't you use the Force?"

Because he was only fourteen, and it didn't come as easily to him. But Ferus didn't want to tell his Master that. "There wasn't time."

"There's always enough time for a Jedi," Siri said. "The point is, the Force is always around you."

Ferus struggled to sit up. He was growing fast, and his legs and arms always seemed to get tangled up underneath him. That's why he had fallen.

"Our bodies aren't just bone and muscle," Siri said. "They're also liquid. And air. And the ground isn't as hard as it looks."

Ferus seemed to feel every bruise. "So you say."

She sprang to her feet, reached out a hand, and hauled him up, laughing. "You make everything harder than it has to be, Ferus. Even dirt."

Ferus felt his body relax. The Force moved through him, and his muscles suddenly felt fluid. He bent and twisted easily and fit into the small space. Then he closed the compartment door and flew upward on a rush of air, so fast that he felt dizzy.

The compartment door opened as he felt himself held up on the zero-gravity field. He pushed himself out and landed on his feet on the floor of the vast Temple kitchen, capable of feeding hundreds of Jedi. Trever was waiting.

"You were right," he said. "That was some ride."

Ferus glanced around. The kitchen had always been a busy place. The Jedi who had an interest rotated their service, and they were all willing to sneak a growing youngling a treat at any time of day or night. Now it was more or less intact, but, like most of the places he'd seen, strewn with debris and blackened by smoke. An attempt had been made in one corner to restore its function. He could see that the stove was working and a table had been cleared and set up for dining. . . .

The Force surged, a warning, only a half second before he heard the door open.

He really had to work on his Force connection. What was the use of a warning if suddenly twenty stormtroopers appeared in your face?

"Whoa!" Trever dived to the floor as blaster fire streaked through the air. Ferus's lightsaber danced, deflecting the bolts.

He spoke urgently under the cover of the noise. "There's another exit by the stoves. Go, now!" He barked out the order, and Trever took off, running in a crazy pattern that made it hard for the stormtroopers to get a fix on him. Ferus retreated, keeping his lightsaber moving, and thinking, as a Jedi would, three steps ahead.

They would follow him into the corridor. He wouldn't be able to lose them, not there. But the library was close by, half-demolished. There would be more cover there. If he could get to the second level of the library, he could get out the back door, and from there . . . from there . . .

Where?

The answer came to him. Yoda's private quarters. Now Malorum's office.

Malorum was away. It would be empty and quiet. And from there they could access files, maybe find a way to get out that they hadn't considered. And he could find out what Malorum was up to. The stormtroopers would never think someone would be stupid enough to hide in the main Inquisitor's private office.

The only problem was, he would have to go through too much of the main hallway to get there. They'd be spotted.

Ferus's mind cleared, and he recalled walking into the Room of a Thousand Fountains. The water system had been destroyed, the upper canopy that had duplicated the sky was tattered and half-falling. Once, that canopy had changed color throughout the day, shading from the pinks of dawn to the deep purple of dusk, as a lighting system mimicked the passage of the sun. Now the damaged canopy revealed the network of catwalks overhead that serviced the laserlights . . .

. . . and connected to the power conduit tunnel that ran in the walls. Smaller than the service tunnels, but built so that a service person could squeeze in to work on the circuits at any point.

Trever waited for him in the corridor. Ferus was a few seconds ahead of the stormtrooper squad. He dashed down the hall. He had no doubt that the officer in charge was calling for backup. Soon the hallways would be flooded with troops.

The stormtroopers burst into the hallway just as they scooted around the corner. Blaster bolts ripped into the walls, sending chunks of stone falling on them like rain.

"This way."

More blaster bolts shuddered down the hallway. They were shooting just to shoot now, even though Ferus and Trever were out of range. It was an Imperial tactic he remembered from his time in the Bellassan resistance — shoot to intimidate as well as kill. Why not? The Imperials didn't lack ammunition, and they didn't care about the physical destruction of property.

The door to the main hallway was jammed. Ferus leaped at it, using both feet and the Force. The door burst open, and he and Trever charged through. With a lift of his hand, he closed it behind them with the Force. Instantly it was torn apart by weapons fire.

Ferus darted out and across the hallway, down a short flight of stairs, and turned off with Trever at his heels. He pushed open the heavy doors to the library.

He told himself not to pause for even a moment to grieve again over the lost treasures here, not to notice as he kicked through the rubble left by the broken statues that had been the likenesses of the great Jedi Masters.

The staircase was gone. He climbed up a stack of rubble instead, Trever scrabbling behind him. They reached the balcony and ran down to the rear door.

He slid it open just a centimeter to look out. This time he had a few seconds to monitor the activity outside. A small knot of officers were walking away down the hall while several stormtroopers marched toward them. He'd have to time this carefully so that the stormtroopers would pass and the officers keep going before he and Trever ran out.

Downstairs he heard the squad searching the library. Any moment now they would appear.

The stormtroopers passed. Ferus and Trever had to take the chance.

Ferus slipped out of the library, Trever as close

as a shadow. The troops didn't turn as they continued down the hall.

Ferus raced the short distance to the doors to the Room of a Thousand Fountains and burst through. Trever ran next to him now, keeping up without effort. At the end of the path, Ferus stopped and released his liquid cable line, grabbing Trever at the same time. The line pulled them to the catwalk above.

"I'm starting to get used to this," Trever grunted as he jumped down onto the catwalk.

There. Ferus saw the small, grated door at the end of an open stairway. He ran up and put out a hand, hoping that the Force would be there. The grated door popped off. He and Trever jumped inside, and he replaced the grate.

The tunnel was dark, but after a moment he could see. Avoiding the circuits and wires, they began to crawl down the tunnel.

"This runs in the wall," he said in a whisper. "So tread lightly."

He pictured where they were now, on the same level as Yoda's private quarters. When he thought they were near the door, he held up a hand and Trever stopped behind him. There was a grate just ahead. Ferus bent down and looked. He was directly opposite Yoda's quarters. He could see the slats of the window blinds. The hallway was empty. He curled his fingers around the grate, ready to ease it off.

Ferus suddenly heard approaching footsteps.

Malorum. Striding in his Inquisitor's robes, an assistant hurrying by his side. Stopping outside the door of Yoda's chambers.

Ferus felt it, a slight disturbance in the Force. Obi-Wan had picked up on what he'd suspected: Malorum was Force-sensitive. He cloaked his own connection to the Force, even though Ferus doubted Malorum was adept enough to feel it.

"Don't sound the general alarm," Malorum snapped. "By all means look, but look quietly. Lord Vader has decided to pay us an unannounced visit. I don't want him to know about this until the intruders are caught."

"Yes, sir."

Ferus felt the dark side of the Force surge in a sickening wave, so powerful he inadvertently shrank back. He knew what it meant.

The Sith Lord had arrived.

CHAPTER SIX

Ferus's breath felt sucked from his lungs. Darth Vader was on the other side of the wall. From his position near the floor he could only see the Sith Lord's boots, but he could hear the rasp of his breath mask.

Their only hope was that Vader wasn't looking for them.

"The situation is normal, you say," Vader remarked in a deep, booming voice.

Malorum had taken a few steps forward so Ferus could no longer see him. "Yes, as you can see. I arrived a day early — I like to do that, surprise them. It keeps everyone on their toes, and it's a good way to learn things that —"

"You came back a day early because I ordered you to. If you can stop complimenting yourself long enough, perhaps you can explain why squads are patrolling the hallways."

"Strictly routine. I believe in constant readiness."

"Malorum, do you think I'm a fool?"

"Excuse me, Lord Vader?"

The power of Vader's anger filled the hallway. "This is a waste of time, and I hate wasting time. I put up with you because you are useful . . . for now. So I give you a choice. Tell me the truth, or continue your lies."

Ferus could almost feel Malorum's calculations. The beat went on a little too long.

"Two intruders were spotted and are being tracked," Malorum finally said. "I assure you they will be found. You see, in a way, this proves the success of my plan to trap the Jedi. One of the intruders has a lightsaber."

"Really."

"So the rumors we spread worked."

"In order for a trap to work it must capture its prey. You do not have a Jedi in custody. Instead, someone is still on the loose."

There was a note of false lightness now in Malorum's voice. "Temporarily, Lord Vader, I assure you."

"Assurances don't interest me."

Lord Vader sounded almost . . . bored. He treated Malorum with contempt. Ferus had heard that Malorum was Lord Vader's special pet, his protégé. Obviously this was a piece of unfounded gossip.

"And I recall," Vader continued, "that you let a Jedi slip through your fingers on Bellassa. And now there is another Jedi somewhere on Coruscant."

"I have a spy who has infiltrated that Jedi's group. I am waiting for a report —"

"Your tedious obsession with trapping Jedi has led you to neglect your orders. I have given you a simple task — to clean up Coruscant, level by level, down to the very crust, until it is totally under our domination. You were to ferret out every possible pocket of resistance. You were to plan a strike and wipe out the Erased. We can't have resisters turning into heroes."

"Now just a minute, Lord Vader," Malorum said. "Coruscant is hardly an ordinary assignment."

"If you are not capable of the job, I'll find someone else to do it."

"Of course I am capable, Lord Vader —"

"Then do it and do it now. You want to rid yourself of intruders? Blow up the Temple."

Ferus stiffened.

"Blow it up?" Malorum asked.

"Why not?"

"But my private office is here! Valuable records would be lost."

"You overemphasize your own importance."

Ferus could actually hear the breath that hissed

out of Malorum's lungs. "I see what you're doing. You're trying to discredit me in the eyes of the Emperor. You want to destroy my work, my files . . ." Then he stopped. "Wait. I see now. You weren't serious."

"Interesting what has just now emerged, isn't it? You have files here that have not been banked with Imperial security? That is a violation of the Emperor's directives."

This is a battle, Ferus thought. *Malorum wants Vader's job. He wants to be the Emperor's pet. And Vader knows exactly what he's up to.*

Now there was an element of smugness in Malorum's tone. "I have permission from the Emperor himself to keep files private that I feel could jeopardize an ongoing investigation."

"Do I need to remind you of your own inferiority?"

Vader's anger served to quash Malorum's assurance. It was a frightening thing to feel it turned on you, Ferus reflected. He was glad he was behind the panel.

"I have no secrets from you, Lord Vader. There are reports that you haven't seen yet, files that need additional notes . . . I have spies everywhere on Coruscant, as you know. Reports on our progress on surveillance in the sublevels . . ."

"At last you're telling me something I want to know."

"Not to mention certain delicate matters I've been pursuing for your sake alone, Lord Vader. For example, the rumors about Polis Massa . . ."

Ferus strained to hear. There it was again — Polis Massa. Something was at stake, something big, but he didn't know what.

If Malorum thought he was going to impress Darth Vader, he was wrong. His boast had the opposite effect. Ferus could feel it now, the slow burn of Vader's rage as it built.

"Lord Vader —"

Malorum's voice was hoarse, as though he was gasping for breath. Still, Ferus could hear the fear in it.

"I . . . beg . . . you —"

A strange thing was happening. The grating in front of Ferus was vibrating. Then the actual wall was vibrating. He heard a cracking sound. Vader was allowing his rage to build.

"Do not ever mention that place again."

"Of course, Lord Vader."

Across the hallway, Ferus could see that the windows of Yoda's quarters were vibrating. Suddenly the door blew in. He saw a chair sail across the room and heard it slam against a wall. Part of the ceiling cracked and cables crashed down.

Ferus signaled to Trever and began to crawl backward.

The windows shattered. The grate blew out, along with a large chunk of the wall. Ferus and Trever were exposed.

CHAPTER SEVEN

Ferus and Trever tried to pull back amidst shards of glass and looked straight up into the black breath mask of Darth Vader. Malorum was hanging in the air, a victim of Vader's wrath, his face almost purple.

Vader released his Force-hold, and Malorum fell to the floor with a croaking sound.

For a moment, no one moved.

Vader looked down at him, and Ferus looked up, and everything inside him dissolved into pure fear. He looked into that black mirrored mask and wondered who the being behind it really was. Half living, half mechanical? He didn't know.

Somehow training kicked in. He had a moment, and it spun out into enough time. Ferus knew he didn't have enough power to fight a Sith. Not even close. But he couldn't let Darth Vader dominate the

Force, either. He reached out for the Force and was hit by a surprising wave. It grew in intensity and power, the most powerful surge he had ever felt, as if Yoda himself was here to help him. It felt almost as though it was *directed* at him, emanating from Yoda's room.

Ferus rode a wave of the Force, grabbing Trever with one arm and jumping out to snatch at the flexible cable that had fallen from the ceiling. It was still attached above, and it gave him something to swing on. Together with Trever he swung out through the broken wall of glass, and then let go. He knew the Force would carry him.

He and Trever soared over the atrium and landed on the other side. He could feel the dark side of the Force behind him, but he paid it no mind. He simply ran, all the while knowing that if Vader wanted him, he would have gotten him. Simple as that.

Perhaps he was letting Ferus and Trever go in order to humiliate Malorum. Or test him. Or because he didn't care that much. Whatever the reason, Ferus grabbed on to it and ran with it.

Alarms sounded.

Now the entire Temple was on alert. Ferus switched to a hallway that he knew was a shortcut to the analysis rooms. It was dark and dusty; the Imperials didn't use it. Using his lightsaber for light, he led the way. This could buy them a few precious seconds. In his mind, he was forming a desperate plan. The only way they were getting out of here was if they did it fast; Ferus knew he wouldn't be able to hide for very long. There was no question that Malorum wouldn't allow himself to fail in front of his master.

"What's the plan?" Trever asked, breathing hard. "The sooner we get away from that Vader guy, the better. Can we review? Scary! Creepy!"

"We have to steal a ship," Ferus said. "The new landing platform lies directly below a playroom that the younglings used. During surveillance I saw that the window is partially blown out."

"I'm sort of sensing that we'll be jumping out a window again," Trever said.

"Well, I'm hoping there will be a nifty little speeder underneath us."

"You know, you keep forgetting something. I'm not a Jedi. I can't do all this leaping and landing."

"You're doing just fine. Hurry up."

Ferus slowed down as they reached the playroom. He crept forward. Just as he'd hoped, the room wasn't being used. A cold wind blew in from the broken window. Followed closely by Trever, he stepped inside.

A wave of horror hit him, hard, directly in the chest.

Something happened here.

The younglings . . .

How had he pushed that thought away? He had imagined, somehow, that the Empire wouldn't target the young. He had imagined the younglings had simply . . . run away.

They did not run away.

Youth, age, the sick, the weak . . . they do not enter into the Sith's calculations. They simply go after what they want.

Don't think of it. If you think of it now, it might break you.

He walked slowly to the window. It felt as though he was kicking through ashes. The toys were still scattered about, the climbing apparatus the younglings had used, the practice lightsabers, the lasertoys, all broken now.

What kind of monster would be capable of this?

Trever lurked behind a fallen column, keeping well out of sight as he spied out the window. "They're closing down the landing platform," he said. "Must be a security measure."

Shaking off the dark memories in the room, Ferus joined him. While they'd been inside the Temple, dusk had fallen. Lights were blinking on all over the levels below them. "Look at that officer, arguing. The code is yellow, not red. See the light at the side of the platform? So my guess is that they let him go."

The Force surged. It was a warning. Ferus was startled at its directness. Much of the time he felt he was groping for the Force through a fog. He realized that his Force connection was stronger while he was here. Something in him still responded to this place, still gained strength from it.

Malorum was close.

He looked around the room. He had seconds. There had to be something here he could use. His mind was working fast. He needed something to distract the pilot below. All he needed was an instant.

He scooped up one of the youngling's toys. It was used for Force practice. In the beginning, the lasertoy would fly in a straight line. As the child grew in expertise, he or she would use the Force to make it dip and roll. The more it cavorted, the more laserlights blinked on and off. Ferus checked it. A few lights blinked at him. It still worked. This little toy had made it through the destruction all around it.

He stood by the broken window. The officer below had been cleared to take off. Ferus let the laser-toy fly.

Now all he needed was the Force.

He felt it flow effortlessly between him and the toy. He sent the toy spinning and diving. The lights blinked and flashed, faster and faster, the colors penetrating the gloom.

The guards below pointed and raised their blaster rifles. He could see that they were puzzled, not knowing what the object could be. Was it a weapon? The pilot hesitated, unsure of what to do.

"Hang onto me like a monkey-lizard," he told Trever.

Trever leaped on his back, winding his long arms and legs around him. Ferus positioned himself on the ledge. Everyone below was looking at the laser-toy. He jumped. The Force helped him slow and guide his descent.

The speeder was still hovering near the guards. Obviously the officer wanted the protection of their weaponry before he took off. Ferus kept the laser-toy spinning even as he guided his leap.

It all happened in less than an instant. He landed on the back of the speeder. Trever slithered off his back and into the backseat.

Ferus picked up the officer under the arms. The officer was too startled to struggle. "I need a ride," Ferus said.

He tossed him from the vehicle. They were still hovering only meters from the platform; the officer wasn't hurt, but he wasn't very happy about his rough landing. He, too, drew his blaster and began firing furiously.

"Time to go," Trever said, ducking under the seat.

Blaster fire streaked around them as the guards realized what had happened. Ferus pushed the engines and they zoomed off.

CHAPTER EIGHT

What now? Trever wondered. With every new idea Ferus had, he found himself spinning in atmospheric storms, dangling from towers, and stealing Imperial speeders. He didn't know if he was having the time of his life or if he was simply crazy for sticking around.

He wondered for the thousandth time why he was here. Every time he had a chance to bolt, he said no.

The truth was, the galaxy became such a big place when you had nowhere to go.

And anything he could do to destroy the Empire that had destroyed his family — he'd do it.

"We know now that Malorum believes the Jedi is alive and on Coruscant," Ferus said. "We'd better ditch this speeder fast and start looking."

"Now?" Trever asked as Ferus piloted the speeder to a landing at a crowded platform. "Don't you ever stop?"

"Not having a good time?"

"Food and sleep would be nice."

"No sleep, not yet. But I can get you some food where we're headed. If he's still there." So much had changed, Ferus thought — he didn't expect anything to be the same. But he couldn't stop hoping.

It was gone. Where Dexter's Diner once occupied its tiny space there was now an empty lot. Ferus stood, looking at the space where it had been. It had been razed. Why?

He didn't know Dexter Jettster all that well. He'd only met him a couple of times. But Obi-Wan had told him to look up Dexter if he ever needed information or help, and to tell him that Obi-Wan had sent him. The fact that Obi-Wan trusted Dexter with the fact that he was still alive meant something.

Ferus kicked at a piece of rubble. He wasn't the only one who knew Dexter Jettster. His diner was known throughout Galactic City. Someone had to know what had happened to him.

A woman in a red cloak passed by and smiled at him. "I've seen that expression on so many faces," she said. "Looking for sliders, right?"

"They were the best in the galaxy. What happened?"

"Disappeared," she said. "Happened the same night the Empire destroyed his diner."

"Why?"

"Accused of subversion, aiding and abetting enemies of the Empire."

"The usual," Ferus said bitterly.

The woman gave him a sharp look. "Be careful what you say," she said softly.

There was a human man walking near them. Probably just someone on his way home after a long day of work. But you never knew who could be an Imperial spy.

Ferus waited until the man had passed. "Do you know what happened to Dexter?"

"Rumors," she said. "Coruscant is always full of rumors. Some say he was arrested. Some say he is dead. Some say he travels the galaxy, just as he used to, going from job to job on energy-harvesting freighters. And some say he's joined the Erased."

That term again. "'The Erased'?" Ferus asked.

She gave him a curious look. "You don't know about them?"

"I . . . I left Coruscant a long time ago."

She gave him an appraising look. "Well, if you're back here, you should know about them. The Enemy Eradication Order of Coruscant was issued shortly after the Emperor took over. It was specifically designed to target those who had been active in the Republic. At first, it was just surveillance. They'd have to check in with an Imperial officer every week.

They were forbidden to travel. But soon surveillance led to arrest, arrest to death or a living death, so . . . some engineered their own disappearance. They help each other now. You can get rid of your name and your ID docs and any record of your existence and simply . . ."

"Disappear."

"As if you'd never been born. They say they live below. Far below, in one of the sublevels."

"I see. I'm glad for Dexter, if he did make it out. He was a friend." Their words had passed back and forth, but something else was going on underneath. She was sizing him up, trying to decide what he was. And he was telling her, with every word, that she could trust him. He knew that she knew more than she was telling.

"It's dangerous," she said. She glanced around furtively.

"Everything is dangerous, these days."

Her brown eyes were wary, and she appeared to make a decision. "My advice, of course, is not to go in the orange district near sunset."

"Thank you for the advice," Ferus said, as she nodded briefly and walked away. Did he imagine it, or did she breathe "good luck" as she passed him?

Most of his missions as a Jedi apprentice had taken him to the Mid-Rim worlds and beyond. He knew that a few of the other Master-Padawan teams, such as Anakin and Obi-Wan, had more experience on Coruscant. Ferus didn't know the underworld of Coruscant very well. But even he had heard of the orange district.

It wasn't an official name. You wouldn't find it on a map. It had gotten that name from the residents' habit of replacing the Senate-issued street glow-lights with orange ones that lent the passages and walkways a lurid air. Every time the officials had changed the lights back to the clear ones, the residents somehow managed to return them to orange, block by block and street by street. At last the Senate had given up on the problem and let the orange district be.

Ferus had never actually been there, but he wasn't worried about finding his way around. This was part of what he did, go into dicey situations and try to find out information without making too many stupid mistakes.

Sometimes he did better than others.

They took an air taxi down to the district. The driver zoomed off as fast as he could. Who could blame him?

There was little illumination here except for the garish laserlights that flashed invitations to various clubs and bars and, of course, the orange glowlights. Down here, it was never silent. The press of beings made walking difficult. Those who couldn't afford the upper levels lived here, in small cubes that passed for apartments in huge structures housing thousands. Many of them, Ferus was sure, were scheming how to make their way to the upper levels to live underneath the sun again.

"Smart," Trever said. "Hide in plain sight. Even the Empire would have trouble tracking someone here. Can you imagine making a house-to-house search? It would take about a thousand years."

They continued down the walkway. Blocks of compressed garbage towered above them. Although it had been sanitized in the processing, it still gave off a faint smell.

"I think I just lost my appetite," Trever said.

"We're in the quadrant now," Ferus said. "And it's sunset."

"How can you tell? It's always orange down here."

Ferus gazed around. He could go into a shop or sit on a bench and wait until someone approached him. In districts like these, beings always had things to sell, and that always included information. But maybe a café was best.

"It's better not to advertise that you're a stranger here, but not seem too at home, either," he told Trever as he looked around. "If we can find a small café . . ."

"Ferus . . ."

". . . it has to be the right one."

"Ferus! Look."

Ferus followed Trever's jerk of his chin. Down a particularly dangerous-appearing alley, a small laser-light hung over a door. It would be easy to miss, thanks to the all-enveloping orange glow in the air. It was a round red light with cracks emanating from it. The cracks made the light appear to be a dying sun.

"Sunset," Trever said. "In the orange district."

"Maybe. Certainly worth a try."

Ferus led the way down the alley. "I'll go in first. You stay out here."

"I'm not sure about this," Trever said. "Maybe I should hit the street, pick up something I could pretend to sell — dataparts, for example, and —

"Pick up dataparts? Don't you mean *steal* them?"

"Don't be so precise. My point is, I'll get inside pretending to be a seller and get a good look around. Nobody ever suspects a street kid."

"No, I'll go," Ferus said. "I've got experience with this. It's got to be some sort of cantina. You can always find someone to help you in a cantina, if you approach it the right way. Wait here."

He pushed open the door . . . and walked straight into the tusk of a Whiphid as it picked him up and threw him out the door.

Ferus landed hard. He felt his side gingerly. The Whiphid had barely nicked him with his tusk. Still, he could feel the burn. Thank the stars for small favors.

Trever strolled over to look down at him. "Oh," he said, "so that's how it's done."

The Whiphid crossed the distance in two gigantic strides. He towered over them. "This is a private club! Get your carcass back to the hole it crawled out of!"

"Hey, Tooth-Face!" Trever shot back angrily. "Who do you think you're talking to?"

"They don't like it when you call them that," Ferus murmured. "So I wouldn't —"

The Whiphid picked up Trever with his clawed hands and tossed him on top of Ferus. Ferus felt his breath puff out in a *whoosh* at the impact.

"Call the garbage compactors!" the Whiphid roared to someone inside. "We've got some trash!"

A slender human male in an ankle-length coat stood in the doorway. Ferus recognized the telltale signs of a slythmonger, a being who bought and sold narcotics and potions, sometimes without regard to whether they were deadly or not.

I can take them both, Ferus thought. *The Whiphid just took me by surprise. I can handle this.*

The slythmonger laughed. "Come on, sweetblos-soms. We've got two live ones!"

A tall Bothan and nine — no, ten — other beings charged out the door.

Okay. Maybe not as easy as I thought.

Trever rolled off him. Ferus sprang to his feet, his hands held up, palms out. "Hey, I'm just looking for some information."

"And what makes you think we have any to give?" the slythmonger asked.

"Not give. Sell."

"He's got credits!" a tall human man called glee-fully. "Get him!"

As if in one mass, the homicidal crew headed toward them.

He didn't want to use his lightsaber. News would get back quickly that a Jedi had been spotted. He didn't want to tip off Malorum. He knew now that Malorum believed Fy-Tor was alive, and that would only endanger her.

Still, he didn't particularly want to get himself and Trever killed.

Trever had the most finely honed sense of self-preservation he'd ever seen. Within seconds, he had scurried over and rolled under a burned-out speeder.

"Wooo," a woman with a crisscrossing holster

packed with blasters yelled. "Look at the little womp rat run! Get him!"

Ferus leaped and landed on top of the speeder. He drew his blaster. "You'll have to get through me."

With a slither and a clatter and a clang, everyone's weapons came out. Pocket blasters. A blaster rifle. Vibroshivs. Vibroblades. And even what looked like an Imperial force pike.

"Gladly," the Bothan said.

Suddenly a deep laugh rolled out from the dark interior.

"Would you mind not killing the poor fellow, chums?" Dexter Jettster said. "I think I might know him."

CHAPTER NINE

Dexter beckoned to them with three of his four hands. Ferus and Trever stepped uneasily into the dark bar. Only a few steps behind them, the disappointed crew followed, muttering darkly about what they'd missed out on.

They sat at a small table that was dwarfed by Dex's bulk. Waving the others away, he fixed his friendly, beady eyes on Ferus.

"Ferus Olin, is it? I remember when Siri would bring you by. And here I thought you left Coruscant behind forever. That would have been a smart move. And who is this with you?"

"Trever Flume," Trever supplied.

"Well, Trever Flume and Ferus Olin, what brings you down to these parts?"

"Obi-Wan said you would help me," Ferus said. "I just left him a few days ago."

Dexter leaned backward. All four hands went to

his chest as he let out a gusty breath. "You should prepare a fellow for news like that. He's alive. That's good to hear. Where is he?"

"I can't tell you that," Ferus said. "But he sends his regards."

"Well, if you see him, tell him Dexter Jettster is still his friend."

"He'll be glad to hear you're well."

"Well?" Dexter chortled. "I wouldn't go that far. Not that far, at all. But I'm surviving."

"You're one of the Erased."

"Erased I am. No name, no background, nothing to declare except — I'm alive." He chuckled again, but this time ruefully. "Obi-Wan spoke too soon. I doubt I have help to give you. But if you've come to be Erased, I can put you in touch with the right channels. I can find you a place to stay for a bit — not too long, because the Erased have to keep moving. Some of us keep track of one another, some of us disappear. There are no judgments down here. Whatever you do to survive, you do."

Ferus glanced over at the long metal bar. The group that had followed the Whiphid outside were lined up against it, their backs to the bar, their eyes on him. The Whiphid stood behind the bar, moving a dirty rag back and forth and watching, too.

"Now, don't worry about them. They're just looking out for me. It's best to intimidate any visitors.

Creatures come down here looking for thrills, and we send 'em back to where they came from. A little worse for wear, but alive. Ha! Ha! If I say you're all right, you'll be welcome enough."

"Who are they?" Trever asked curiously.

"A mixed lot, I'd say," Dexter answered. "Anyone the Empire was hounding. Heroes and villains. Some journalists, some former Republic army officers. Maybe some criminals mixed in."

Ferus gave a sidelong glance at the slythmonger. "I noticed that."

Dexter slapped both knees with four hands. "Hah! You're speaking of Keets."

"Yeah, the one who couldn't wait to run us through with a vibroshiv," Trever said.

"Ah, his growl is worse than his chomp," Dex said. "And he wasn't a criminal in the old days. He was a journalist, writing for the *Coruscant Holo Net*. One of the first to ask why Palpatine was grabbing all the power even while he was smiling at us, telling us he was protecting us."

"Not Keets Freely?" Ferus asked, astonished. He had read Freely's commentaries during the Clone Wars.

"The very same. And the Bothan fellow with the tangled mane — that's Oryon, one of the best spies the Republic ever had. The human female with the spiked hair-horns? Rhya Taloon, the Senator from

Agridorn. Can't go back to her homeworld — she's got a death mark on her head. So she escaped. See that Svivreni? He was a Senate aide. And the tall humanoid? An officer in the Army of the Republic. Not a clone. Don't ask about the brothers — the ones standing next to each other who look alike? They haven't told us who they are."

Ferus looked around the room again, this time in surprise. "Here it is," he said, excitement underneath his words. "Right here, in this room. Seeds for the rebellion. Here is where it will begin, in places like this."

Dexter laughed. "We're a long way from rebellion, young Olin. We're just trying to survive. Coruscant used to be a decent place to live, if you didn't mind a billion beings breathing your air. Things have changed. There are spies around, of course. But even ordinary Coruscanti just trying to get by are having a real hard time. Bribes and intimidation — that's a way of life now."

"We were just at the Jedi Temple," Ferus said. "We've seen the damage there."

"They say there are Jedi imprisoned there."

"There aren't."

"Didn't think there would be. That's why I warned the other one."

Ferus's alertness sharpened. "What other one?"

"She didn't give me her name."

"A Jedi — a human woman, with a small facial marking on her forehead —"

"That's the one. She heard I'd been a friend to the Jedi and sought me out. That was before I Erased myself. I couldn't give her much — I was surprised that any Jedi was alive at all. But I did tell her not to go to the Temple. She went down below instead, into the deepest sublevels."

"Do you know where, exactly?" Ferus asked.

"No idea, my friend. But recently I got a message. If I ever need her, she said, I should look for Solace."

"Solace?"

"A word I've been hearing more and more lately."

"But where is it?"

Dex shrugged. "Don't know. I haven't needed her yet."

Ferus looked around. "There's something you should know. The Empire is planning a strike down here. They want to wipe out the Erased. You're all becoming bothersome to the new regime. They want to control Coruscant all the way down to the crust."

Dex stroked his chin with his thick, gnarled fingers. "That won't be easy, even for the Empire."

"Darth Vader has made it his personal mission."

"Darth Vader? That's another story." Dex frowned

in thought, the deep furrows in his face collapsing until his eyes disappeared. Then he looked up again at Ferus. "You'll need a guide if you're going below."

"Do you have someone in mind?"

"Maybe, maybe. But first, a small parley with the gang."

Dex signaled to the others and they retired to another room in the back of the cantina. It turned out that the building was an old relay power station, and it still held abandoned turbines. The Erased had hooked up their own power system here, and the air was filled with steam and a constant humming noise.

"Makes it hard for surveillance to get a fix on voices," Dex explained to Ferus and Trever. "You've got some here who are a little touchy about being overheard."

Seven of the Erased sat at the table along with Dex. The others had melted away, not even willing to sit and talk with outsiders. The Whiphid stayed at the bar.

The Erased all turned to Dexter to begin, and Ferus realized that he was a kind of unofficial leader here.

"My friend here is Ferus Olin, a former Jedi."

"Jedi apprentice," Ferus corrected.

"And this is his friend . . ."

Trever chimed in with his name.

"Ferus tells me that the Empire is planning to try to eradicate us, and I trust his information," Dexter continued. "We all knew it would happen. Just sooner than we'd like."

"We're not prepared for this," the Svivreni said. He was stocky, with a narrow, furred face. His hair reached the back of his knees and was held back with a thick metal band.

"This is Curran Caladian," Dexter told Ferus and Trever.

"I knew a Tyro Caladian," Ferus said. Tyro had been a friend of Obi-Wan's, and a good source of information. Ferus had met him a number of times. He had been one of twenty-one beings killed in the great Senate massacre, a few years before the Clone Wars began.

"My cousin," Curran said. "We started out as aides at the Senate together." He gave Ferus a look of recognition. "You were there that day — at the massacre. You saved Palpatine's life."

Ferus nodded. He had reasons to remember this. He knew now that he couldn't have possibly saved Palpatine's life that day. Palpatine, he felt sure, had been supremely in control at every moment, had perhaps even foreseen the attacks and turned them to his advantage. Certainly his courage under fire had netted him more supporters than ever.

"Is that so?" Dex slapped four hands on his massive legs. "If only you'd moved a little to the left that day, Ferus, we all might be in better shape! Ha!"

Ferus acknowledged the joke with a slight smile. He felt that nothing he could have done that day would have made a difference.

"Back to the subject at hand," Dex said. "Or hands. Seems to me we have some decisions to make. First, we should warn the others. Everyone is on their own, of course. But if some of us can help, we should help."

"Help how?" The tall man who Dex had called a former officer spoke up.

"Offer the Erased a place to go if they need it. Leave the orange district."

The man nodded. "We've got to go deeper."

"I agree with Hume," Rhya Taloon said. Ferus could not connect the image of this woman, her silver hair twisted into horns, holsters crisscrossing her chest, with the image of a Senator.

"Our strength lies in our bond," the Bothan Oryon said. "We should find a place we'll all be safe. Not just us, but any Erased who wish to join us."

The two young men who Dexter had referred to as brothers sat together. They followed the conversation carefully, looking from one speaker to another at the same moment. They nodded in agreement.

"Gilly and Spence are right," Dexter said, even though the two young men hadn't spoken. "Now what about Solace?"

Rhya Taloon spoke up. "I've heard rumors about it. A kind of refuge, they say. Secret. Safe. Impossible to find, yet many find their way there."

"I say we find it," Dexter said. "Ferus has got the skills to protect us on the journey."

Me? Ferus thought. *Since when did I volunteer?*

Keets Freely gave a long look around at the sweeping machines, the pools of rusty water, and the grimy walls. "And leave all this?" he joked.

Wait a second, Ferus thought. *I thought I was getting a guide, not leading a group.* He shot a look at Dexter. His eyes were twinkling . . . if you could say such a thing were possible for a Besalisk's beady eyes.

Oh, well. He'd been outmaneuvered. But he didn't mind doing Dexter a favor. He'd do it for Obi-Wan's sake. And to help find the lost Jedi.

Trever didn't mind. That was clear by the grin on his face. He liked these people. No doubt they reminded him of the black marketers he lived with on Bellassa.

"Take a vote, then," Dexter suggested.

Slowly, weapons were raised. All seven Erased agreed to go.

"I'll be staying here," Dex said. "I'm not as

77

mobile as I was. I'll warn the others to stay low —
well, lower than normal — and I'll wait to hear
from you."

As they went to collect their weapons and
belongings, Ferus talked to Dexter.

"Don't think I didn't notice how you trapped me
into this," he said.

"Where's your spirit of adventure, young Olin?"
Dexter chortled and slapped him on the back, sending him shooting forward. He saved himself from
crashing into a column just in time.

"I should tell you something, Dexter. If you're
relying on the skills of a Jedi, I dropped out of the
Order some time ago. I'm a little rusty."

"I'd rather have a Jedi at half-power than a bat-
talion of stormtroopers any day," Dexter assured
him. "And call me Dex. I have a feeling this is the
beginning of a long friendship."

The Erased left to gather the few belongings
they needed to take, and Ferus took the opportunity to gain some privacy and contact Obi-Wan. He
withdrew into a little-used part of the space and
took out his comlink.

They had agreed on a coded signal before they
parted, and Obi-Wan answered at once. A flickering
mini-hologram appeared, and Obi-Wan flipped back
his hood.

"News?"

"Hey, Obi-Wan, glad to see you, too."

Obi-Wan frowned. "You are supposed to contact me for emergencies only."

"Well, it's not an emergency, so I guess you don't want to hear what I have to say. Bye!"

"Hello, Ferus," Obi-Wan said wearily. "How are you?"

"Nothing a few days of rest on Belazura wouldn't cure. I'm here with your friend Dexter Jettster. He sends his regards."

"Dex! I'm glad to hear it."

"He's got a death mark on his head, but he's alive. Listen, I broke into the Temple with Trever and overheard something of interest about Polis Massa."

Obi-Wan straightened. "Yes?"

"Darth Vader doesn't care about it. Whatever it is. In fact, he forbade Malorum to pursue any inquiry."

"That's good."

"No, that's bad. Because Malorum is trying to become the Emperor's right-hand man and boot out Vader. So he's going to pursue it."

"Do you know what he knows?"

"No, I didn't get that far. The wall caved in."

"You have to find out. You must be alert for any inquiry into the death of Senator Padmí Amidala as well. Do you think you could get back into the Temple?"

"Trever and I barely got *out*."

Obi-Wan folded his hands into the sleeves of his cloak. "You know I can't leave here, Ferus. And I don't want to put you and Trever in danger. But Malorum has to be stopped."

"I'll stop him for you, Obi-Wan," Ferus said. "I don't know how, I don't even know why. But I'll do it."

"May the Force be with you."

"You know, I'm beginning to realize that it actually *is* with me. Still."

"Of course it is, Ferus." Obi-Wan's voice was warm now. "Depend on it."

CHAPTER TEN

For the first time since he'd left the streets of Bellassa, Trever felt at home.

The Erased reminded him of the friends he'd made in the black market. Sure, you didn't want to ask the brothers, Gilly and Spence, what they did before they were Erased, but that was fine with him. He was used to people concealing their pasts.

Gilly and Spence didn't say much. They were short and compact and heavily armed with various makeshift weapons they trusted more than any blaster. Keets Freely was the talkative one. That guy could chew your ear off with facts about the Coruscant underlevels: How they'd always existed outside of the law. How security didn't penetrate this far down. Millions of inhabitants relied on their own defensive skills or teams of vigilantes to protect neighborhoods and individual apartment structures with their hundreds of inhabitants.

According to Keets, ever since the Most Evilest Empire took over, things had only become worse. Before the Clone Wars, the Senate tried to keep the place from falling apart, at least. They sent droid teams down for occasional repairs. They even set up med clinics for the poor slobs who had to live there. But now, with the new greedy Senate, nobody cared. So the millions of beings slammed into the sublevels traveled in packs and kept arsenals of weapons to protect themselves.

Trever could have skipped the lecture and picked up the main point — watch your back.

He noticed that Ferus wasn't too happy about leading the Erased down. They had traveled for hours until they were far away from the Senate and Galactic City, and all Ferus could think about was the Jedi he was searching for. Honestly, he was a little obsessive about it. But still, Trever had never met anyone he felt he could depend on like Ferus. It was worth sticking around.

Their plans were loose. They had to be. The group had decided to head down, all of them packed into one large speeder, and pick up information along the way. Since there were so many rumors about Solace, they felt certain that they would find the way there.

Of course, some of the rumors were pretty extreme.

Number one: Solace was a place on the crust

that had escaped the monolithic building boom on Coruscant. It had trees and lakes and was open to the sky far above, with nothing on top of it.

And if you believe that, Trever thought, *you believe in space angels.*

Number two: Solace was built centuries ago on the crust, a wondrous place of palaces and towers where all were welcome, and all were cherished, and all were free.

Right, and the Emperor is a humble guy looking out for everyone's well-being and the galaxy is a blooming garden.

The only rumor Trever truly believed was the fact they already knew: Solace was hard to find.

At the end of a long day of learning basically nothing, Rhya Taloon unstrapped her holsters to make herself comfortable and stretched out on the sleep couch in the guesthouse they'd arranged to stay in for the night. Gilly and Spence were busy cleaning their weapons while Trever lay down on the other sleep couch, and Ferus spread his cloak on the floor for a bed.

"This is getting us nowhere," Rhya announced to the ceiling. She placed the toe of her boot on the opposite heel and kicked off one boot, then the other. They landed with a thump on the floor.

"You've got to ask a lot of questions before you

get real answers, sweetblossom," Keets said as he sat astride a chair. "We may not see it, but we have pieces of the puzzle."

"We do?" She waved a hand in the air. "All I heard today was noise."

"There's one thing we keep hearing. The crust. It's all the way down — some say it's even *below* the crust."

"That's true," Ferus said. "That's the common thread."

Oryon shook back his tangled mane of hair. He was in his usual resting position, squatting on the floor. It looked uncomfortable to Trever, but Oryon seemed to find it relaxing. "There is usually a kernel of truth in even the most exaggerated rumor. Keets might be right."

Gilly and Spence looked up from their weapons to nod.

"There's got to be a first time," Hume said. He was the tall human man who'd been a Republic army officer.

Keets saluted him. "Even a broken chrono is right twice a day."

"So we should go straight to the crust," Curran said. "Stop wasting time."

"Sounds like a plan," Hume said. "I hate to waste time."

Everyone looked at Ferus. "I agree," he said.

"Anybody ever been that deep before?" Keets asked.

"Are you kidding?" Rhya asked. "I never made it out of Galactic City." She looked down at the holsters on the floor. "Then again, I never shot a blaster before, either."

Orvon checked his weapon. "Well, get ready. You might have plenty of opportunities soon."

They left for the crust at first light.

They zoomed down past sublevel after sublevel. There were no space lanes here, just tricky piloting. Ferus piloted the speeder, not speaking, concentrating on avoiding the other aggressive speeders he encountered as well as broken sensors that suddenly loomed in front of him, crumbling landing platforms, and narrow passages.

Coruscant had been built from the surface up. When the levels had become too crowded to bear, more levels were built above. More buildings, more infrastructure, more power stations, more walkways. The deeper Ferus and the others went, the more ancient these structures became.

They left the speeder on a landing platform that had been shored up with timbers of durasteel and wood. Looking around, Trever could see that improvisation was the name of the game when it came to building down here.

Here at the crust, they entered a century that was committed to grandeur. These long-ago beings built their buildings out of stone, hundreds of stories high, with intricate carvings and balconies, turrets, and towers. The stone of the buildings was cracked and crumbling. Often they were reinforced with scrap metal or wood. Their streets were winding and narrow, with alleys leading off from alleys in a confusing maze.

There were no official systems here at all — no power, no water, no light, no ventilation that wasn't powered by private generators. They walked down through a narrow arched walkway. The stone beneath their feet was cracked and split, sometimes with fissures that were meters wide. They jumped when they had to and skirted the holes. They were the only beings out on the streets. Although above them the suns weren't setting, it felt like night. The air was dark and close.

This was it — the bottom of Coruscant. The lowest known level.

If they didn't find Solace here, there was nowhere else to go.

Trever hoped there was safety in numbers. The Erased looked treacherous. He couldn't imagine that anyone would want to tangle with them.

He found his steps slowing. He felt haunted by what was above. It was as though he could feel the pressure of the millions of lives above him, the millions of structures and machines, a whole impossible matrix of humming life above his head, of millions of beating hearts.

It was enough to seriously creep him out.

"You're uncharacteristically silent, young fellow." Keets fell into step beside him.

"It all feels so . . . heavy," Trever said.

"You mean everything above your head?" Keets laughed. "Yeah, I see what you mean. It's kind of oppressive."

"So who lives down here?" he asked.

Keets shrugged. "Immigrants from other worlds, those who came here hoping to do better. Those who lost everything, those who had nowhere else to go. Just creatures living, trying to live. And those who prey off them."

"And those looking for the wonderful world of Solace," Trever said.

Keets chuckled. Then suddenly he reached over and pushed Trever hard. Trever fell to the rough ground.

"Hey, what —"

Then he saw them. The gang had materialized, seemingly out of thin air, but Trever now saw the narrow passageway that snaked off the arched walk. Keets had pushed him out of the way of a stun dart just in time. Trever looked up and saw that Oryon had already reached for his light repeating blaster from his back holster. Keets held a blaster pistol in his hand. Now Trever saw the streaks of blaster fire in the darkness, a steady barrage, as the gang moved forward. There were at least fifteen of them, each more brutal-looking than the rest.

Ferus was already running, his lightsaber sweeping in a continually moving arc. The attackers were clearly startled at the ferocity and power he exhibited, not to mention the blaster fire that suddenly boomeranged back at them. They kept firing as they retreated, shouting curses at Ferus and promising to kill him.

Oryon and Hume kept up a position on Ferus's flank, each of them firing their weapons. Keets and Rhya were only slightly behind, while Gilly and Spence split up and began to chase the gang as they gave up firing and fled.

Trever started to roll to his feet. The fissures and cracks were wider here, and his foot became lodged in a crack as he moved. Annoyed, he tried to pull it out, but it was stuck. Trever squirmed closer to peer into the crack.

A thick, scaly tail had wrapped itself around his ankle.

Trever gave a yell of surprise and tried to pull his leg up. The creature wound another length around his ankle and tugged. He tried to kick at it, but it only hung on tighter.

"Ferus!" Trever called. But Ferus was ahead, with Rhya and Hume, and didn't hear him.

He looked down again, and this time he saw the dead eye of the creature staring back at him. He didn't think that the concept of mercy existed in this creature's universe.

It gave a sudden yank, and Trever dropped into the crevice up to his hips. His other leg now dangled inside the crack, and he pushed away the question of whether this creature had a mate. He kicked and twisted, hitting the creature now with one fist while with the other hand he fished for something — anything — in his utility belt.

Trever felt the familiar contours of an alpha charge.

His fingers fumbled as he tried to set the charge. He managed to do it, but the creature tugged, and the charge rolled out of his fingers and dropped into the blackness. In the flash of light he saw a reptilian body with scales that looked like duracrete. The mouth of the creature appeared to be strong enough to snap him in two.

Suddenly something whistled by his ear. He caught the glint of a vibroshiv as it wheeled through the air in a spinning, perfect aim for the tail. It sank in up to the hilt. The thick tail suddenly unfurled, and Trever heard the sound of the creature slithering away.

"Duracrete slug," Keets said, holding down a hand for him and hauling him up. "About ten meters long, by the look of him. They burrow into the stone. Best to keep an eye out."

"Thanks for the tip." Trever dusted off his pants.

Ferus hurried over. "What happened?"

"Nothing much. I was almost strangled by an enormous slug. Nothing for you to worry about," Trever said. He didn't know why he felt so irritated that Ferus hadn't saved him. Ferus had been walking ahead, not concerning himself with Trever at all.

"Hey, sorry. Thanks," Ferus said to Keets.

"Sure. You owe me a vibroshiv." Keets grinned, his teeth white through the dirt streaked on his face.

"We found a place that might provide some information," Ferus said.

The others had paused in front of two crumbling stone columns. A sputtering laserlight sign read: UNDERWORLD INN. They regarded it as Ferus, Trever, and Keets walked up.

"Not your most premier establishment," Rhya said.

"We do need a bed for the night," Ferus said.

"And where there's beds, there's grog," Keets said. "And where's there's grog, there's gossip."

"Let's give it a try," Ferus said. "But keep your weapons close."

They pushed open the stone door. They walked into a large circular space formed by towering arches. The stone floor and stone ceiling made their footsteps echo. Huge alien gargoyles leered over their heads with what looked like malicious intent.

"Homey," Hume remarked.

They approached a small battered desk that was dwarfed by its surroundings. A clerk sat behind it, fast asleep. Ferus cleared his throat, but he didn't stir.

Oryon slammed the hilt of his blaster rifle down on the desk, and the clerk awoke with a start. "Fire!" he shouted.

"No fire," Ferus said. "Just some customers."

"Oh." The clerk straightened. "Ah, we only have a couple of rooms available. You'll have to double up."

"Fine."

"Costs extra for towels and water."

"Extra for water?"

"Hard to get water down here."

"All right, all right."

Ferus was about to produce his false ID docs, but the clerk waved a hand to dismiss him. "Just credits. We don't need ID docs."

"I thought it was the law."

The clerk raised an eyebrow at him, as though Ferus was a new recruit into a very old army. "There's no law down here. If you haven't figured that out yet, I feel sorry for you."

They paid the credits, and then Hume asked, "We've got some dry throats here. Any recommendations?"

The clerk shrugged a shoulder in the direction of a doorway.

They pushed open the door and went inside. The cantina was small but the ceiling was high, casting deep shadows throughout the space. To Ferus's surprise, the place was almost full. Humanoids and other creatures sat at the bar or at small tables that hugged the shadows. Weapons were prominently displayed on the tables.

"Reminds me of a place I used to go in Galactic City called the 'Dor, only worse," Keets observed.

Ferus nodded. He'd been to the 'Dor with Siri, as a Padawan who had tried very hard not to be intimidated by the atmosphere. The dregs of the galaxy went there to drink, buy or sell information, and hire bounty hunters. It had once been called the Splendor until most of its laser letters had shorted out, and everyone just called it the 'Dor.

"I'd say we should have a seat," Hume advised. "We're attracting a bit of attention here."

"Not necessarily a bad thing," Oryon said. "It might get us some answers."

They took over several small tables and ordered drinks and food. They saw that they were being observed. Ferus took a small sip of his drink, then got up and brought it to the bar to see if anyone was in the mood to chat. Meanwhile, Keets struck up a conversation with the table next door.

They ate the food and finished four pots of tea and talked to almost every person in the bar, but no one was able to get directions to Solace. Everyone had heard of it, but no one knew where it was. Finally, the cantina cleared out and they had to admit defeat. Trever had been feeling woozy for some time. He yawned.

"We might as well get some sleep," Ferus said.

The room was large, with sleep couches and one receptacle and outlet that dribbled pale yellow water. The couches were just planks with a blanket on top. Not the most uncomfortable bed Ferus had ever slept on, but it was definitely in the top ten.

He turned on his side and looked at Trever's tousled hair sticking up from his blanket. He felt bad about not being the one to help Trever earlier. He'd made sure Trever was safe during the battle, then concentrated on their attackers. He had heard

Trever's cry, but by the time he'd started to run, Keets was already there.

He couldn't be there for him every time. Or so he tried to tell himself.

He didn't know where his responsibility to the boy began or ended. He knew, of course, that Trever was hardly as self-sufficient as he professed to be. Even though the boy had lived on his own for years, he occasionally needed guidance, someone to watch over him.

Was that his job?

If he were still a Jedi, if the galaxy hadn't changed, he'd be old enough to have a Padawan now. But Trever wasn't his Padawan. Ferus didn't have the connection with him that a Master Jedi would. He didn't have the link that he'd had with Siri. He lost track of him occasionally. And he couldn't tell what he was thinking or feeling.

It was better that they part, that he find a haven for Trever so he could grow up safe and secure. Even loved, if that were possible.

Because Ferus would just keep burying them deeper into complications and danger. It wasn't fair to Trever. Today it had been a ten-foot duracrete slug. But what would tomorrow bring, and the day after that?

With those disquieting thoughts, Ferus felt himself slipping toward sleep. The soft breathing in the room told him that the others had succumbed, despite the hard, flat beds.

Suddenly he heard a noise. Ferus put his hand on his lightsaber, but soon saw it was Trever, crawling toward him quietly so as not to awaken the others.

He stopped by the head of the sleep couch, his eyes gleaming.

"I know where to find Solace," he said.

CHAPTER ELEVEN

"It was when the slug started to pull me down —"

"Trever, I'm sorry I —"

"Enough with the guilt wallow, Feri-Wan — I'm trying to tell you something. I dropped an alpha charge and when it went off, the light showed me something. More than a ten-foot predator chewing on my ankle, I mean. There's something down there."

"Something?"

"Something more than a duracrete slug nest. I was thinking about it. There was a glint . . . like there was metal or something, or water. I'm not sure, but it was like there was . . . space. Like a room. Or something. It's just that . . . remember when some of the rumors said *below* the crust?"

Ferus didn't have to ask if Trever was sure. He trusted this boy's perceptions.

"I'll wake the others. Let's go."

*　　*　　*

It was now what many called the empty hours. Too late for even those who walked these dangerous areas at night, too early for those who rose before dawn. They kept close together as they walked.

Trever led a yawning Keets and the others to the spot where the duracrete slug had tried to pull him through the crack. Ferus leaned over and shined a glowlight down into the space. He couldn't tell, but he thought Trever was right — there *was* something down there.

"I think I can fit," Ferus said. "Let me go down, and if I see anything, I'll call up."

Keets leaned against a column and yawned. "Take your time."

Ferus eased into the opening. There was a crumbling half-wall once he got below, he saw. It was deeply gouged with the tracks of a slug, but that gave him toeholds and handholds. To his surprise, Trever began to climb down after him.

"Stay up there," Ferus told him.

"No way. I found this place, I'm coming."

Ferus knew it would be a waste of breath to argue. He continued to climb down slowly. He jumped the last few meters. His boots hit solid ground. Trever jumped next to him a moment later. He held a glow rod over his head for illumination.

Ferus could see now that they were in a tunnel.

Gigantic blocks of stone formed the walls and ceiling. The floor was deeply grooved and he could see the remnants of machinery buried in the tracks.

"That's what you saw glinting," he told Trever. "This must have been some kind of transportation system."

He shouted up to the others that the way was clear, and they began to climb down, one after the other.

Hume avoided a steaming yellow pool that released a rank odor. "Careful," he said. "Looks like some toxic waste down here."

"The system must have been primitive," Rhya said. "They used rails for transport."

Keets looked up. "There are still conduit lines in the ceiling. I wonder where they lead."

"It sure doesn't look like Solace," Hume said. "But the tunnel could lead us there."

Ferus heard a whisper above. That was his only warning as a black shape suddenly dropped from the ceiling into their path.

He didn't have time to grab his lightsaber hidden in his cloak. That's how fast the creature was.

He was a short being, with compact muscles, and wore a close-fitting helmet over his features. His waist was tightly cinched with a belt that held a variety of weapons. He didn't assume a threatening pose, however. He seemed casual as he watched them move closer, the Erased all holding their weapons and training them on him.

"You mentioned Solace," he said.

Ferus nodded, watching him warily. "We want to go there."

Gilly and Spence moved to the man's rear, and Keets, Oryon, Hume, and Rhya moved in even closer. The intruder didn't seem rattled in the least.

"I can take you," he said. "It will cost you."

"Why should we trust you?" Trever asked.

"Because your choices are limited here at the crust," he replied. "Either find it yourself, or use me."

"How do we know you can find it?" Keets asked.

"Because I've been there. I'm the only one who's been there and has come back."

They knew part of what he said was true. They had heard of those who'd gone to Solace, but they'd never heard of one who had returned.

"You've got to do better than that," Ferus said.

"What many don't know is that long ago, before Coruscant was a city-world, it had vast oceans," the intruder said. "The oceans were drained and pumped into caverns below the crust. That's where you'll find Solace."

The others exchanged glances. It sounded real

to them. It made sense. That was why it was safe, why even the Empire would have a hard time finding it.

"What's your name?" Ferus asked.

"Just call me Guide," the intruder replied. "I left my name behind long ago. Like you, I have wiped out all traces of my past."

Something is off here, Ferus thought. There was something odd about Guide. But then again, there was something odd about everyone down here.

Guide was right. They didn't have much choice. It was the only lead they'd found since they started. Slowly, Ferus nodded.

"Take us there," he said.

CHAPTER TWELVE

Guide held up a glowlamp. "Best to keep close down here. Watch out for duracrete slugs. They're especially aggressive."

"I think we've already been introduced," Trever muttered.

They kept to the middle of the tunnel as they walked. The walls dripped moisture. Occasionally they would pass a reeking toxic pool, glowing strangely in the darkness. They heard slithering noises, but no creatures appeared.

"The original cities of Coruscant were built on the crust, centuries ago," Guide explained as they walked. "Much of the infrastructure is still underground. Most of the water and power tunnels have caved in, but there was a people-moving system that relied on some sort of primitive engine that connected to a track in the ground. These tunnels were built out of blocks of stone, and some are still intact.

Later they were used to pump the oceans into the caverns. That's where we're going."

They walked until they lost a sense of where they were and whether it was day or night above them. Ferus began to feel the lack of sleep and decent food. He pushed on.

Suddenly he heard the echo of lapping water. Guide stopped. "The water will grow deeper, but we'll come to catwalks that will take us above it."

Soon they splashed through ankle-deep water. Up ahead he saw a crude stairway, and as Ferus followed the stairs with his eyes he saw that it connected to a series of platforms and more stairs. When Guide reached the stairs, he began to climb.

They climbed from platform to platform in the darkness. Ferus didn't know how deep the water was below them, but he could sense it. It was almost as though it still had tides, for it seemed to roar and recede as though it were constantly moving. He couldn't see it, he could only smell it and hear it now.

They heard a splash and looked over the side. Far below they could just make out a huge sea creature turning and slipping under the water again.

"Oh, yes," Guide said. "I should warn you — don't fall in."

The scaffolding suddenly opened out into a wide space that ran the width of the cavern. Planks of plastoid and wood were laid in a pattern. Structures had been built in separate circular encampments that connected to each other through metal walkways. It was like a small city.

In several of the structures Ferus saw lights come on. Whoever was inside was waking up.

Guide held up a small device, and an electronic noise pinged.

The denizens began to emerge from the structures. They were from many worlds, and all were armed with weapons. They slowly walked toward Guide.

The Erased found themselves pressed together in a small group as the settlers ringed around them.

Ferus began to feel uneasy. They were completely surrounded. Outnumbered.

A murmur began, some words passing from being to being. Guide held up a hand for silence.

"I brought them to you from above," he said.

Then he suddenly turned on his heel and merged with the crowd. "They are yours now."

The crowd began to move closer. Ferus, Trever, and the Erased backed up. But there was nowhere to go. Only the thin railing of the catwalk, and the long drop to the black ocean below.

CHAPTER THIRTEEN

It wasn't as though he didn't see this one coming from a kilometer off. Ferus had been poised for Guide to betray them. He would have been stupid not to expect it.

But it turned out he was foolish anyway. He had thought Guide might lead them into an ambush of some kind. He didn't expect the ambush to come from the members of Solace.

"Solace takes care of us," a woman said.

"Solace brings us what we need," someone called.

They were talking about Guide, Ferus realized. Solace wasn't a place — it was a person.

This was how they survived. They were scavengers. They spread the rumor of Solace above, and when Guide led a group back, they stole from them and used their credits or items of value to buy supplies. That was all painfully clear.

He felt the steady support of Keets, Oryon, and the others next to him. Trever's fingers appeared to be hooked into his belt, but Ferus knew he was fishing for a small explosive device. Maybe a smoke grenade.

The first line of settlers charged. Trever tossed the grenade, and the smoke rolled toward their attackers. At the same moment, Ferus drew his lightsaber, ready to deflect the blaster bolts he was sure would be streaking toward him.

He saw someone somersaulting through the smoke and air, and he held his lightsaber ready.

"Wait!"

The command came from Solace, who landed directly in front of the group. Everyone froze.

He walked forward. It was so quiet they could hear his boots click on the walkway.

He came close to Ferus, so close the glowing tip of the lightsaber was only millimeters from his chest.

"Jedi," he said.

"Unfortunately for you, yes," Ferus said.

Solace held up the glowlamp and examined Ferus's features. "Not quite, I think."

"Not quite what?" He wasn't supposed to be having a conversation, he was supposed to be fighting, but he certainly didn't mind the delay. It gave him more time to look for openings, avenues of escape, individuals who looked more competent than others, hidden weapons.

"You should have done that already, Not-Quite-a-Jedi," Solace said. "You should have done it the first moment you arrived."

"Are you giving me lessons?"

"Obviously, you need them. *Padawan*."

Admittedly, Ferus's instincts seemed to fail him at the worst times. But he suddenly understood what was off about their guide, and what he should have guessed all along.

"You're Fy-Tor," he said. "You're a Jedi."

"It's about time." Their "guide" slowly removed his helmet. Ferus recognized her now. Fy-Tor had pitched her voice deeper, moved differently, but he knew her.

She was gaunt, her cheeks hollowed. Her forehead marking was still there, but it was faint now, a faded tattoo. She had shaved her dark hair, but her blue eyes were still piercing.

She held up a hand.

"These are not for you," she called to the settlers. "Disperse."

The crowd melted away, except for one man who remained a few steps behind her. His hands rested on his thick utility belt as though he was prepared to defend Fy-Tor at any moment.

She spoke to him without turning. "Donal. Can you get Ferus's companions some food? They've been walking most of the night."

"Of course."

"No one will hurt you now," she told them.

The Erased moved off, but Trever stayed stubbornly by Ferus's side.

Fy-Tor raised an eyebrow. "Your apprentice?"

"I wouldn't say that," Ferus said.

"Me either," Trever said.

"We've been looking for you, Fy-Tor," Ferus continued.

She held up a hand. "Don't use that name. I've left it behind. I'm Solace now. You left the Jedi. Some sort of spat between Padawans, I heard."

A *spat*? Ferus remembered the depths of his heartache, his guilt. "Hardly a spat."

"So you say. Where did you find that lightsaber?"

"It was a gift from Garen Muln. The Jedi you left in the cave at Illum. The one you said you'd return for."

"I tried."

"So you say."

They faced each other, close to adversaries now. Ferus didn't know how it happened, but it had. He wouldn't back down, although he could tell she was waiting. Either she still thought of him as a Padawan, or she was used to subservience from the settlers here. That was apparent in the way she gave orders, the way she expected them to move when she told them to move.

"I see we're off to a good start," she said. "Come on, Olin, let's sit and you can tell me why you were looking for me. Step into my office."

She sat astride a bench fashioned from what appeared to be a reclaimed speeder seat. Ferus sat, too. Trever crouched on the floor. The expression on his face was wary; he didn't trust Solace yet. Neither did Ferus. The reunion he'd imagined taking place had been filled with relief and emotion, the core of understanding between Jedi. This wasn't even close. Solace was unreadable to him, and she seemed to have no wish to connect, Jedi to Jedi. Instead, so far she'd taken every opportunity to remind him that he wasn't one.

"I know of another Jedi who is alive, besides Garen," Ferus said. Although Obi-Wan had given him permission to tell other Jedi that he was alive, Ferus elected to wait with details until he had a better grasp of what Solace was like. He was still bothered by the fact that she had led them here and then turned her back indifferently to their fate. Whatever had happened to her had pushed her very far from the Jedi path.

"He is in exile, but Garen and I have established a secret base for any Jedi I can find. If we gather together again, we can become stronger."

Solace took this in. "You're serious? You're going to travel the galaxy, picking up stray Jedi — who may not even exist — and bring them to some camp?" She gave a bark of a laugh. "Count me out!"

"If we stay together, we'll be better able to fight when the time comes."

Solace shook her head. "The galaxy is controlled by the Sith. They've killed us all. Your plan is doomed, Ferus, and I want no part of it." She spread her arms. "I've got everything I need here."

"Beings who worship you," Ferus said. "Yes, I can see you have all the attention and service you could want."

She refused to be baited. "What's wrong with that?" she asked. "I've taken those who the Empire would have squashed like slugs and given them a safe place to live. What makes you think your plan is so much better than mine?"

"We were destroyed," Ferus said quietly. "Betrayed. Even our younglings were slaughtered. What makes you so indifferent to that?"

Solace looked away, down through the grating to the ocean below. "Those were black days, and I don't choose to revisit them."

"Someday we can rise against them," Ferus said.

"I believe that with my whole heart. And if I can help in any small way, protect even one Jedi, then I've pledged myself to that."

"May the Force be with you, then," Solace said. "But I'm not going anywhere. I've got a good deal here. I go on the occasional bounty-hunting job to finance this place. It's filled with beings I trust. The Empire doesn't know where to find me. It doesn't even know I'm alive."

"I'm afraid they do," Ferus said. "Trever and I broke into the Temple and overheard the head Inquisitor Malorum with Darth Vader. Vader knows you're alive, though he doesn't seem to care much. He's a Sith."

"There are always two," she said. "I didn't know who they were, but of course that makes sense."

"Malorum knows you're alive, too. He's planning to take back the sublevels of Coruscant, to go all the way down to the crust. That's why the Erased came down here — to see if they'd be safe. But Malorum also mentioned that he'd planted a spy near you."

"A spy? Here? I don't believe it."

"I don't know if it's true, I'm only telling you what I heard. He could have been trying to impress Vader." Ferus waited a beat. "But can you take that chance?"

Solace didn't answer.

Ferus leaned closer. "They've kept the light-sabers."

Solace looked up.

"Hundreds of them. Maybe more. From the Jedi they killed."

She clasped her hands and leaned forward, resting her forehead against them.

"They're lying in one of the storage rooms, gathering dust."

"What do you want from me?" she asked.

"I'm only here to find a Jedi. . . ."

She took another breath, then lifted her head. "We should go back to the Temple."

Ferus wasn't expecting this. "What?"

"We'll get inside and find out what they're planning, for the settlers here and for the Erased."

"I don't think we can," Ferus said. "The security will have been tightened."

"We'll steal the lightsabers back. If, as you say, there are more Jedi alive, we'll have lightsabers for a whole army, if we need it. In any case, you can hide them. They shouldn't lie with the Sith." Her face hardened. "It's a . . . desecration."

"I agree, but —"

"And I'll discover who the spy is, if there is one. Too much is at stake. We can leave immediately."

"Solace, wouldn't it make more sense to abandon this place and leave Coruscant altogether? Even if you don't want to come to the asteroid, the galaxy is a big place. You can find somewhere to hide."

"I'm tired of running. They've driven me here. Here is where I stay."

"We just left the Temple a few days ago. I don't think it's possible to get in and get out now. Let alone navigate once we're inside. They'll be on full alert."

"Double full *extra* red alert," Trever put in.

"How did you get in?" Solace asked. Her face was intent. Ferus saw that she had already made up her mind.

"Through one of the towers, then down through the service tunnel to the main building."

"The hard way."

"I didn't say it was easy."

"Why didn't you go through the supply turbolift shaft along the southeast wall?"

"There is no supply turbolift shaft on that side."

"Of course, you don't know about it. . . . It was built during the Clone Wars. We had so many more pilots, so much more gear to move back and forth to the hangar. The main shaft runs vertically up from the storage areas and then connects to a horizontal shaft that runs to the living quarters. Was that part of the Temple destroyed?"

"No, it's been damaged, but much of it's still intact."

Solace reached into her belt and withdrew a small device. She sent a holographic map spinning into the air. It was a schematic of the Temple.

She pointed. "You see? The shaft is here and runs from the base of the building. You can connect to the horizontal shaft here. Then it connects to the main turbolift shaft in the spire."

"The spire is damaged."

"I know, but it doesn't matter. They probably don't use this turbolift. There's no reason to — it mainly served the living quarters and the hangar. Where is Malorum?"

"In what used to be Yoda's quarters."

"Then his office is here. It's only a short distance from the shaft."

Ferus felt his blood quicken. Was it possible? But he shook his head. "Even if we could use the new turbolift, how will we get in?"

"I have a way. Unlike most of the buildings at that level, the Temple was built by sinking pillars into the crust. I've found those pillars. We can follow them up to the base. Then we can break right into the new turbolift shaft."

"Through the floor?"

"We'd have to blast it," Trever said. "They'd be on us in seconds."

"No, I have a different way." Solace sprang to her feet. "Let me show you."

They stood in front of a small, two-person craft. It was the oddest thing Ferus had ever seen. It looked like an ARC-170 with a cut-off nose. Devices he didn't recognize were set into the hull.

"I can see it's a vehicle, but I can't figure it out. Looks like it could be an interceptor, but . . ."

Solace grinned. "I started with a shell and built it myself. It's a hybrid — a fighter with a mole-miner capability. I bought the mole miner and took out the plasma jets. They're mounted below. I had to remove the shields and the laser cannons, so I lost some defensive and offensive capability, but it's still fast. The ship can burrow through solid rock. It can get through the base of the Temple, I promise you."

"But why did you build it in the first place?" Ferus asked.

"I live under the crust. I need an exit strategy. So, what do you say? I'm going. Are you in or out?"

Ferus looked at Trever. It might be foolhardy, but it might be brilliant. They could steal back the lightsabers. They could raid Malorum's files. He could find out what Malorum had learned about Polis Massa. He could find a way to stop him, follow through on his promise to Obi-Wan. This could be his only chance.

"I'm in," he said.

CHAPTER FOURTEEN

"You're not going without me," Trever said.

Ferus's expression clearly said *not this again*. But Trever didn't care. He wasn't going to be left behind. He'd been left behind before. By his mother, by his father, by his brother. Each time, they'd said *It's too dangerous. You'll be safe here*.

Each time they said *I'll be back*.

"It's a two-person ship," Ferus said. "There's no room. I'll be back —"

"No! Don't say that," Trever warned. "Just . . . don't. I can help. I've been to the Temple. I'm small — I can get into tight spaces. And you'll need some blasting expertise."

Solace looked at him doubtfully, and he bristled.

"I've got half- and quarter-alpha charges, and I've made my own mini-blasts," Trever said. "No noise, no smoke, just sweet entry anywhere you want to go."

Solace looked at Ferus.

"Trever has had an interesting history," he said.

"If we take the tool kit out, you can fit behind the seat." Solace looked at Ferus. "The kid can handle himself. You could, too, at his age. So relax."

"Ferus doesn't know the meaning of the word," Trever said.

Solace and Trever laughed, and some of the pressure Ferus felt inside eased. It was good to be laughed at again. It felt like friendship.

Hume, Rhya, Keets, Oryon, Curran, Gilly, and Spence were sitting at a table fashioned out of a slab of permacrete balanced on some old protocol droid legs. Ferus approached them and sat.

"I'm taking off. Solace promises you'll be safe here. Her assistant Donal will look out for you. I don't think I'll be long. Solace and Trever and I have decided to break into the Temple again. This time, I'm going to get a look at the files and see exactly what Malorum is planning. Unless we go, this place won't be safe."

"We'll come with you," Hume said.

"No. First of all, there's no room. And second — well, you came with me to find Solace, and you found it. This is my battle."

Ferus stood. He looked at each of them. They'd been together only a short time, but he felt tied to them, tied to their struggle to stay alive.

It was Curran who spoke up, using the words of the Svivreni. On their world, it was considered bad luck to say good-bye.

"The journey begins," Curran said softly. "So go."

When Ferus returned, he found that Solace had already done the preflight check. Trever had squeezed into the space behind the seat. Ferus slid into the passenger seat directly behind Solace. The craft was so small that they easily navigated through the cavern and zoomed into the underground tunnel.

"I've explored all through the tunnels down here," Solace said. "There are more than I told you about. It took me months to get all the parts for this craft and build it."

She piloted through the tunnel, flipping the craft sideways when she had to. Then she zoomed up through a huge crack in the ceiling and they entered the main lane of the old city on the crust. They buzzed through the empty place.

"The columns for the Temple were sunk near the tech warehouses," Solace continued. "They were hard to find because the trash heaps were built around them about a century later."

After maneuvering for nearly an hour, the craft dipped down into a vast smoking heap of garbage piled hundreds of meters high. Solace navigated the space, veering around the piles. At last they saw a thick column ahead, and then another, and another. "There are the supports. Hang on."

Now they were going straight up, hugging the column as it rose through the sublevels of Coruscant. Trever fought against dizziness. He was looking straight up through the cockpit canopy. Level after level rushed at him, floors, spires, walls, walkways, lights, beings, cloud cars, air taxis, landing platforms.

It had taken them so long to get down to the crust, and now it was all receding behind him so quickly.

The buildings grew more thickly around them. Lights came on. Dawn was breaking above them. Speeders and air taxis streaked past them. And they were still below the surface.

He knew they were close when Solace pulled back on the speed. "Our best chance is to do this quickly," she said. "In and out."

Above them Trever saw the base of the massive Temple building. Even down here he could see evidence of damage, blackened stone and missing chunks, as though the building had been hacked away at.

Slowly they cruised around the base, searching for the place Solace was looking for. She positioned the ship's nose against the wall. A whirring noise began, and the plasma jets began to slice through the base.

Fine dust coated the windshield, but Solace had thought of that, too. A rotating device cleared the windshield every few seconds, leaving them complete visibility.

The plasma jets cleared a hole just big enough for the ship to get through. They flew inside and found themselves directly in the turbolift shaft.

"It worked!" Solace exclaimed.

"I wish you didn't sound quite so surprised," Ferus remarked.

"Malorum's office first. Then back down to storage if we haven't been discovered."

The craft ascended the shaft, then turned into a horizontal turbolift corridor. They could see the turbolift itself now, unused, at the end of the shaft. Beyond it they could see that the corridor had been blasted, some of it caving in. The turbolift was partially destroyed.

Solace gently brought the craft to rest on the shaft flooring. The cockpit canopy whirred back, and one by one they climbed out.

"This lift door opens out into the service hall-way," Solace said in a low tone.

She and Ferus stood by the door. Trever watched them. Something was passing between them, and he supposed it was the Force. He couldn't feel it, but he was starting to recognize its presence, just by the quietness that surrounded Ferus when he accessed it. Then, without a word being spoken, Ferus stepped forward and cut a hole in the door with his light-saber. They stepped through.

The hallway was empty. Trever followed behind as the two Jedi moved quickly and silently. He almost tripped on a conductor wire, but caught himself just in time. He broke out into a sweat at the thought of the noise he would have made if he fell.

In and out, Solace had said. *Attract no attention.*

This hallway had been used recently. He saw evidence of scrape marks along the power vents, as though they'd been pried off. Was the Empire look-ing for something hidden in the Temple? They'd heard the same rumors he had about treasure being kept here. Of course, according to Ferus, Palpatine had started the rumors, but that didn't mean Imperial officers knew that.

Why had there been conductor wire on the floor?

Ferus accessed a doorway to the main hallway.

Trever could see the door to Malorum's office. It was open. They could hear the sound of others in the building, but the hallway was clear.

Quickly they crossed the hallway and went into the office. Ferus hurried to the desk.

"The holofiles — they're gone. So are the data-pads."

Solace looked around. "It's been cleaned out."

"I guess Vader wanted Malorum back under his nose."

"I won't learn the name of the spy now," Solace said in disgust.

Ferus frowned. He went to the window and looked out, keeping out of sight. "Where are the troops?" he wondered. "This place was crawling with them when we were here last. You'd think there would be even more."

"Something's wrong," Solace said. "I feel it."

"I feel it, too."

"Let's find the lightsabers and get out of here," Solace suggested.

The glowlights dimmed for a moment, then resumed. It was just a glitch, Trever told himself. But something was making him uneasy. Something that had nothing to do with the Force, and every-thing to do with the Empire.

The wire he'd almost tripped on. The scratch marks on the power vents.

"Wait," he said.

He whipped out his servodriver and hurried to the power panel. He unscrewed it from the wall and looked inside.

"Trever, what is it?"

"Power leakage," he said. "Something is sucking the power from the core generator."

"Why?"

"I can think of only one reason," Trever said. "A version of a sleeper bomb. They've tapped different power stations, all at once, to fuel it. They're draining the power to build the explosion. They've gone into different power vents. I'd say they wanted to tap enough power to blow the entire Temple."

"It's Malorum," Ferus said. "That's why he cleared out his office. Vader told him to do it, so he's doing it. Even though Vader wasn't serious. It's Malorum's way to disgrace Vader in the eyes of the Emperor. He can claim that Vader gave the order."

"Do you have any idea when it could blow?" Ferus asked Trever.

"It's just a guess," Trever said. "But if that glitch means what I think it means, we could have just made the shift to reserve power."

"Which means what?" Ferus asked.

"Which means soon. Minutes." Trever swallowed. "We don't have time to leave the way we came."

"We could go out the front entrance," Solace said. "Take our chances. Leave the Temple and let it be destroyed."

"I can't," Ferus said.

Solace nodded. "Neither can I."

CHAPTER FIFTEEN

They raced through the main hallways. There was no time for subterfuge.

Malorum and his officers had withdrawn most of the stormtroopers, but they had left attack droids to continue the patrols, to prevent interference from intruders. Ferus bounded toward the first group as it wheeled to engage them. His lightsaber moved rapidly as he mowed through them from one side while Solace took the other. She was all movement and no wasted motion, her lightsaber a blur. She was faster and better than Ferus and together they destroyed the droids in only seconds. They met in the middle and raced through the gap they'd created, smoke rising around them. Trever kicked through the hot metal and followed.

They knew where the central core generator was. The only chance they had was to shut it down before the bomb was fully armed.

Not trusting the turbolifts, they swung down-stairs, leaping down and letting Trever catch up when they had to pause to dispatch more attack droids. They made it to the power source, a white room where the mighty sublight generator hummed. The reserve power light was blinking.

"Here's the bomb," Trever said, hurrying over to it. "They didn't bother to hide it. You've got to shut down the main generator. But do it gradually, or it could trigger the bomb."

"Thanks for telling me." Ferus turned his attention to the power-core controls. He knew how to do this. He had made it a personal course of study to find out how the infrastructure of the Temple worked. Quickly, he accessed the power computer bank. He went through the necessary series of steps to shut down the system. He went slowly, powering each subsystem down from green to yellow to red.

The lights flickered and failed. They heard the gentle sigh as the air system shut down.

"What now?" Solace asked.

"We wait," Trever said. "And hope we don't blow."

Solace held up her lightsaber, which gave a soft blue glow. Trever got out his glow rod. The seconds ticked by. He looked at the power indicator on the bomb. Slowly, the indicator began to move.

"It's draining," he said. "It won't arm." He looked up at Ferus. "You can kill it now. It's dead."

Ferus swiped a clean strike through the bomb. The device split into two neat halves.

"How long before they figure it out?" Solace asked.

"Soon," Ferus said. "I would imagine that Malorum is nearby. He'll want to see it blow."

"We stopped him this time. But all he has to do is set another one," Trever said.

"I think Vader will find out and stop it," Ferus said. "That's my guess, anyway. Word will get back. If the Emperor wanted the Temple completely destroyed he would have ordered it done. He wants it to remain. It's a symbol to the galaxy — the wreck of the Jedi Order. But to us, it's a symbol of what we can be again."

"I don't know if it's a symbol of anything anymore," Solace said. "I just know it was my home, and I don't want them to blow it up."

They walked out of the central power control center and started down the hall again. Suddenly they heard the noise of stormtroopers clacking down the hallway. Ahead, from this vantage point, they could see the entrance to the Temple. As they looked, the doors flew open and stormtroopers poured in. Malorum was at the head. They could hear his voice boom, bouncing off the high stone walls.

"Find them!" he screamed.

A sea of white flooded the main hallway. They turned and ran. They could not meet this display of force. Overhead, seeker droids began to fan out, searching for them.

They ran back the way they had come. They had to get to Solace's ship. It was their only hope for escape.

Pursued by a seeker droid, they raced down the hallway. Ferus leaped and twisted, slicing it in two.

They could hear the stormtroopers behind them, running now. "They must have picked us up on surveillance," Solace said.

They had seconds. Ferus hurried Trever through the hole to the turbolift shaft. Solace followed. Blaster fire peppered the lift door as Ferus stood, deflecting it. When he was sure Solace and Trever were inside the craft, he turned to leap inside the hole.

At that moment, at least fifty more stormtroopers appeared, some of them on AT-RT walkers. If Solace waited for him, they would all be captured or dead.

He looked at Trever, whose eyes were wide, pleading. "I'll be back!" he yelled.

"I told you not to say that!"

Ferus deactivated his lightsaber and lifted his hand. Solace saw his intention and leaped up momentarily to catch it as it flipped through the air. He would allow himself to be captured, but not his lightsaber.

"Now go!"

Solace hesitated. He saw how close she was to joining him. He couldn't let her.

"You've got to get him out of here!" Ferus shouted.

As Trever screamed and hammered her back with his fists, Solace pushed the controls, and the ship took off.

It had all taken less than a moment. He knew Malorum would want to take him alive. Ferus turned toward the onslaught, defenseless now, and alone.

CHAPTER SIXTEEN

He sat in a prison. Somewhere. He hadn't been taken off Coruscant, he knew that much. He had a bruise on the back of his head where they'd hit him with a stun baton. His legs still tingled from the blow to the back of his knees.

It was only the beginning, he knew.

He had been in an Imperial prison before and had escaped before they tortured him. He didn't think he would be that lucky twice. The last time, Malorum had been the head officer.

One thing you really didn't want, Ferus reflected through his crashing headache, was an Imperial Inquisitor with a grudge.

He lifted his head when the doors swished open. Malorum walked in. Ferus could feel his enjoyment of the situation. Ferus decided then and there that no matter what they did to him, he was going to give Malorum a hard time.

"We've got to stop meeting like this, Malorum," he said.

"Very amusing."

"No, I mean it. We really do. You've just got to get out of prison. See the galaxy. Have some fun —"

"I'm having fun right now. I'm enjoying this immensely."

"Wow, me too. At last, we're bonding."

"So let's talk."

Ferus nodded and stretched out his legs. The pain nearly made him wince, but not quite.

Be a Jedi, Ferus. Be the Jedi you never were, for star's sake. Accept your fear and find your center.

"Let's talk about the Jedi. I underestimated you, Ferus. I thought you left them and never looked back. But you've been doing nothing else but trying to save them. Who is the Jedi you were with at the Temple?"

"I was with thousands of Jedi at the Temple. And it was so long ago . . ."

"You know what I mean. Today. When you broke into Imperial property. What is the name of the Jedi you were with on Bellassa?"

Ferus pretended to frown. "Funny, he never mentioned it."

"You never caught his name?"

"He never dropped it."

"I find that hard to believe."

"Now there's the difference between you and me. I find it absolutely believable. If all your friends had been wiped out, do you think you'd be going around telling people your name? I don't think so. You'd keep it to yourself, I think."

"If I was a coward."

"Ah, in my opinion, cowardice is underrated. It keeps you alive."

"Is being alive so important to you? That's a pity."

"Are you feeling sorry for me now? I didn't know you cared."

Malorum laughed. "You think I haven't seen this before? Bravado in the face of certain death? You'd be surprised how often those about to die put on a show. You aren't unique."

"I don't care much about being unique. Remember, I was raised a Jedi."

"Yes, you're all the same, I suppose. Hypocrites. Hungry for power. You were about to take over the Senate, you tried to assassinate Emperor Palpatine . . . all while wearing those Jedi cloaks of humility. It was a good scam, but it's over."

Ferus waved a hand in the air. "I love the rhythm of the party line. Just say the lies loud enough and long enough and put a drumbeat behind it, and the next thing you know, everyone is singing the same tune."

"The truth is that —"

"The truth," Ferus said quietly, "is that the Republic is now an Empire, and power is consolidated in the hands of one man. He will do anything to keep it, anything to make it grow, and you are his lackey."

"This isn't a debate. As you say, it's been fun, Ferus Olin. But if you aren't going to cooperate —"

"You have ways to make me talk? Let me think. Torture is still against the bylaws of the Senate. Last time I heard."

"Then you're wrong. The Senate approved the Emperor's call for more freedom in how he handles enemies. In times such as these, extreme measures can be called for."

And so the Senators continued to give the Emperor anything he wanted, Ferus thought. He was changing the galaxy, breaking the covenants the Senate was founded on, and they were voting yes to it. The Sith was clever. Always he acted with the "approval" of a Senate that could not say no.

"I'm sending you to a prison world where no one goes. And if you don't reveal the name of the Jedi you know are alive, you will be executed for crimes against the Empire. Do you think anyone will care? They've already forgotten your name on Bellassa."

"Well, I never call, I never write . . ."

"I'm talking to a dead man," Malorum said. "And it's time for my lunch."

With the same indifference he'd shown throughout the interview, Malorum turned and walked out.

CHAPTER SEVENTEEN

As soon as Solace had landed the ship in its parking place tucked under the cavern wall, Trever vaulted forward and slapped his hand on the cockpit canopy release. Even as it opened, he clambered out over her.

"You left him! You just left him!" he shouted. "It's your fault they caught him!"

"He gave himself up, Trever," Solace said, jumping off the ship and landing lightly next to him. "There was nothing I could do. He left me no other choice."

"Jedi don't leave Jedi!" Trever felt his fury take him over. "But you do, don't you? Twice that I know about. You don't know anything about loyalty!"

Solace stood, impassive. He couldn't tell if she was angry. She didn't seem angry. He wanted her to be angry, he wanted to fight.

"My choices are not your business," she said.

"*Ferus* is my business," Trever said. "He's my friend."

"We'll find him," Solace said. "Wherever they take him, we'll find him."

Trever heard her words as though from a distance. They didn't make sense for a moment. "What?"

"I said we'll find him. I won't stop until we do. This isn't over. But first we need supplies and information. I have to —"

Solace suddenly stopped. She appeared to be listening, but there was nothing to hear.

"Solace, what —"

She turned and ran, silently and swiftly, along the catwalks. She made a leap so impossible that Trever knew it was Force-assisted, vaulting over the catwalks to gain time.

He ran after her, his feet pounding up the stairs. He was halfway to the settlement when he heard it. Blaster fire. Screams.

A bloodied Keets appeared above. Suddenly he was hit from behind and tumbled off the catwalk. He landed at Trever's feet, his body twisted, blood pooling from a wound.

Solace's assistant, Donal, ran toward the edge of the catwalk.

"We're under attack!" he screamed.

Solace was right, Trever thought. *This isn't nearly over.*

He readied himself for the fight. . . .